HOME FOR THE HOWLIDAYS

THE KINGS: A TREEMENDOUS CHRISTMAS
BOOK 3

CHARLIE COCHET

HOME FOR THE HOWLIDAYS

Copyright © 2023 Charlie Cochet

http://charliecochet.com

Cover Art Copyright © 2023 Reese Dante

http://reesedante.com

Edited by Stacy Sirkel

FOUR KINGS SECURITY UNIVERSE

Welcome to the Four Kings Security Universe! The current reading order for the universe is as follows:

FOUR KINGS SECURITY UNIVERSE

STANDALONES
Beware of Geeks Bearing Gifts - Standalone (Spencer and Quinn. Quinn is Ace and Lucky's cousin.) Can be read any time before *In the Cards*.

FOUR KINGS SECURITY
Love in Spades - Book 1 (Ace and Colton)
Ante Up - Book 1.5 (Seth and Kit)
Free short story

Be Still My Heart - Book 2 (Red and Laz)

Join the Club - Book 3 (Lucky and Mason)

Diamond in the Rough - Book 4 (King and Leo)

In the Cards - Book 4.5 (Spencer and Quinn's wedding.)

FOUR KINGS SECURITY BOXED SET

Boxed Set includes all 4 main Four Kings Security novels: Love in Spades, Be Still My Heart, Join the Club, and Diamond in the Rough.

BLACK OPS: OPERATION ORION'S BELT

Kept in the Dark - Book 1 (Standalone series can be read anytime)

THE KINGS: WILD CARDS

Stacking the Deck - Book 1 (Jack and Fitz).

Raising the Ante - Book 2 (Frank and Joshua)

Sleight of Hand - Book 3 (Joker and Gio)

THE KINGS: WILD CARDS BOXED SET

Boxed Set includes all 3 main The Kings: Wild Cards books: Stacking the Deck, Raising the Ante, Sleight of Hand, and bonus story In the Cards.

RUNAWAY GROOMS SERIES

Aisle Be There

THE KINGS: ROYAL FLUSH

Dealing Him In

Calling His Bluff

THE KINGS: A TREEMENDOUS CHRISTMAS

Not So Silent Night

Sleigh It Ain't So

Home for the Howlidays

Rebel without a Claus

CHAPTER ONE

"I'm pretty sure Clara asked us to decorate the Ice Castle, not make it visible from *space*," Sacha grumbled as he added another layer of icicle lights to the roof of the building.

Thankfully, the Ice Castle was only one story and didn't require Sacha to get into the knuckle boom again. Seeing his boyfriend up that high made Gio nervous, even if Sacha had been more excited than concerned.

"Well, no one is going to miss it, that's for sure," Gio replied as he held Sacha's ladder. He was ready to be done, and although Sacha had suggested he go inside numerous times, Gio wanted to help. With only Ace and Sacha putting up the lights outside and everyone else focused on the larger task of decorating the interior of the Ice Castle, the two needed a hand, so Gio stayed.

They'd gotten an early start, planning to get as much done as possible before guests filled the town and flocked to Mugs and Kisses, the town's café. After hours of hanging lights, they were nearly done. As much as they enjoyed the snowy holiday, they weren't used to the biting cold, which had forced them to take more breaks than expected.

It might not be snowing, and they were bundled up from head to toe, but several inches of snow had fallen during the night, and brief intervals of snow flurries fell throughout the morning. They had to finish before the sun set and the temperature dropped.

Decorating the Ice Castle was the final step in helping Winterhaven pull off another successful holiday season. When Colton surprised their family with a Christmas vacation, they'd had no idea a terrible snowstorm had swept through Winterhaven, wreaking havoc with the town's shipments and causing damage to the main building where they held all the indoor festivities.

Thanks to Leo—who'd reminded them they had the resources to help—Mason and Lucky had repaired the damage to the Ice Castle roof while Jack restored the electricity. Colton had used his shipping connections to deliver everything the town needed in time to kick off the holiday celebrations. They'd all pitched in, helping the townspeople decorate the main street, town square, and market stalls. With the only thing missing being the guests, Gio stepped in to do his part.

"I can't believe you booked an entire vacation lodge," Ace said, fastening another row of lights to the roof. "That's awesome, Gio."

Gio saw it as helping. "They're an amazing group of volunteers who are passionate about helping others. I've worked with them for years. They're what keep our organizations going, so I wanted to do something nice for them." When Fitz asked him if there was a way he would be able to help Winterhaven, he'd realized he could help the town *and* show his volunteers that they were appreciated.

"And that's why you're a keeper," Ace said, winking at him.

"He is. Now, can we finish this?" Sacha asked. "I can't feel my fingers anymore. And I'm wearing gloves."

Ace opened his mouth, and Sacha narrowed his eyes, receiving a quick nod.

"Yep, we're done."

Sacha descended the ladder, jumping off when he reached the bottom, his boots sinking into the snow. He turned and smiled up at Gio, stealing his breath away. Sacha was a beautiful, complicated man with a sharp tongue and a wicked sense of humor who most would describe as "grumpy," but that was because he felt deeply. He was soft, sweet, and had a big heart, even if he didn't always know how to express what he felt. Gio cherished being on the other end of that gorgeous smile. Snuggling under the covers with Sacha on a frosty winter morning quickly became Gio's favorite thing.

"Well, hello." Gio pulled Sacha into his arms and kissed him, the warmth of his mouth a stark contrast to their chilled skin.

Sacha hummed before pulling back. He bit his bottom lip, his eyes on Gio's mouth. "We, uh, should go inside before our tongues freeze together."

Gio couldn't argue with that. Sacha grabbed the ladder, and they headed inside the Ice Castle, the warmth from the heating so lovely. The place looked fantastic. So different from when they'd first stepped foot inside. It had been dark and cold, and an absolute mess. Now it looked like a storybook palace that belonged in a snowy European village, with its white walls, blue and gold accents, and sparkling chandelier lighting.

The Ice Castle had been cleaned and decorated beautifully with lush frosted garland and delicate blue and white baubles. There were several rooms, with the largest being the main ballroom. Each room would host a different festive event until New Year's Day, from baking contests and cookie and ornament decorating to card making and, on Christmas Day, meeting Santa and his reindeer.

With the boisterous laughter and noise coming from the main ballroom, it was easy to find the rest of their family. Together with the town's residents, they were almost done decorating most of the Ice Castle's interior, except for the main ballroom and one of the smaller ballrooms, which Clara had informed them was closed for an upcoming private event.

As soon as they stepped foot inside the room, they were bombarded by wiggly furry butts, wagging tails, and happy dog smiles. Gio had released Cookie from his service dog duties, letting him go inside with Chip and Duchess. No matter how excited and happy the snow made the dogs, they weren't used to the cold either.

Even so, Chip, Cookie, and Cocoa seemed to be loving every minute of it. Duchess enjoyed it until she'd had enough, then she searched for the nearest warm spot. Right now, she was curled up in a fluffy bed near Fitz, who sat next to Jack, running his fingers through Cocoa's fur as the puppy dozed in his arms. With all the lights going up, Jack had started programming them for various events, so they flashed in time to the music or whatever was happening.

When Gio became part of this amazing, quirky family, he'd been worried for Jack and Fitz. Everyone at Four Kings Security worked hard, but Jack had taken his responsibilities to an unhealthy level, and it had started to hurt those who cared about him. Gio understood because he'd been the same before losing his heart to Sacha. Gio was relieved that, like he had, Jack finally realized what he'd been doing to himself and his relationship.

Gio shoved his hat and gloves into his coat pocket before taking it off and dropping it on the growing pile strewn across the enormous red velvet couch to the side of the room. After a few belly rubs, Cookie decided to go off and play with Chip, his fluffy tail wagging happily. They darted off to be with Leo, who sat cross-legged on the floor with his laptop. What was Leo up to? He'd been secretive since they'd arrived, and no one knew what was happening. Not even

King knew, but since King wasn't worried, neither were the rest of them. They'd find out eventually.

Ace stopped next to Gio, his hands planted on his hips.

"It's a thing of beauty, isn't it?"

Gio nodded. "The ballroom is starting to come together."

The vast ballroom had a giant Christmas tree with twinkling white lights positioned between the white and gold veined marble pillars lining the left and right sides of the room. The red velvet curtain along the back wall matched the curtains on the arched windows that lined both sides of the room. The marble floor gleamed, and the colossal gold chandelier above their heads twinkled like a starry night. It was beautiful.

"No, I meant all the glorious Christmas sweaters," Ace said, sweeping his arm out toward their family and the unique attire on display. All of which had been, of course, Ace's idea.

The previous Christmas, Ace came up with a different version of Secret Santa that only involved Christmas sweaters. The rule was that they would all pick a day to exchange gifts, and everyone would have to wear their sweater the whole day.

Coincidently, King had gotten Ace as his Secret Santa two years in a row.

"Again, I'm going to say I didn't agree to this," King grumbled as he walked by carrying a box of decorations, his scowl telling everyone who his Secret Santa was. Actually, his Christmas sweater sporting the giant head of Nicolas Cage wearing a Santa hat made it clear who was behind the gift. Ace laughed and hurried after King, undoubtedly to bestow more Nicholas Cage impressions upon his disgruntled brother.

Gio leaned into Sacha. "Why do I get the feeling Ace is somehow skewing the odds in his favor?"

"Oh, you know Ace cheats his ass off," Sacha replied. He dropped his gaze to his own Christmas sweater. "I think I lucked out with Keanu Reeves Jesus."

Gio chuckled. "Well, Keanu does seem like a pretty great guy."

"I could have gotten Lucky's pink candy cane flamingos. Though he looks like he's embraced it. You never know with him."

Lucky didn't seem bothered by his festive flamingos as he handed Mason another section of garland for the pillar they were decorating. The two were often off on their own, and it was sweet. Gio had seen them tucked away, kissing on more than one occasion. Anyone who saw the way they looked at each other could immediately see how in love they were. Gio hadn't been around when the two had gotten together, but Sacha said it had been explosive.

"Colton was obviously Ace's Secret Santa," Sacha said with a snicker. "Who else would get Ace an 'It's not Christmas until Hans Gruber falls from Nakatomi Plaza' Christmas sweater?"

Gio wasn't sure who drew his name, but he was pretty pleased with his Elf "Son of a Nutcracker" sweater.

"Leo got the coolest one," Sacha added, nodding toward Leo. "That Spidey Christmas sweater is pretty badass."

"Agreed."

Last year, the week before Christmas, they all got together to exchange their Secret Santa gifts. So, this morning after breakfast, they'd gathered in the cabin's living room where Leo and Fitz had handed out the wrapped sweaters.

For all of the griping and groaning, everyone had fun unwrapping their gifts. Well, maybe *fun* was too strong a word where King was concerned, but the rest of them had had a good laugh.

They joined Colton in the middle of the room

where he stood with a tablet. King was usually the one who gave the orders where his brothers-in-arms were concerned, but when it came to wrangling *everyone*, including the Boyfriends, King handed the reins to Colton and stepped away, far far away. As the CEO of a worldwide shipping company, no one was better at wrangling cats than Colton.

"The lights outside are done," Sacha told Colton. "We're at Griswold level out there, thanks to your husband."

Colton chuckled. "I'm sure if you'd let him, he'd have found a way to add more, so thanks for reigning him in."

"My pleasure. So, what's next?"

"Mason and Lucky are working on adding garland to those pillars," he said, pointing behind him. "Can you and Gio start on the ones on the other side? Each pillar has a box next to it with everything you'll need. The garland is pre-lit."

"Awesome." Sacha headed for the pillar, and Gio followed. Festive holiday music filled the ballroom, the scents of Christmas in the air. Gio couldn't help but grab Sacha's hand and pull him behind the large pillar.

"You know everyone can still see us," Sacha said, one thick brow arched, but his big blue-gray eyes sparkled with mischief. Oh, how Gio loved this side of him.

"I know." It didn't stop Gio from pulling Sacha into his arms and kissing him deeply and thoroughly. He loved how Sacha's more petite frame fit against him and how he gave himself over completely. Trust was something Sacha didn't give freely. Knowing he had Sacha's trust and his heart was everything to Gio.

Sacha hummed and melted against Gio, the same as he always did. "You're evil." He sounded breathless, his gaze on Gio's mouth.

"Me?"

"Yep. Because all I want to do is climb you like a tree, and instead, I have to climb *that*." He motioned to the pillar behind them.

Gio chuckled. He brushed his lips over Sacha's and slid his hands down to Sacha's ass, squeezing it. "More to look forward to later then." It had been almost two years since they'd started dating, and sometimes Gio still couldn't believe Sacha was his. After everything they'd been through....

For years, Gio had been curious about Sacha, enthralled by his sexy voice. While Gio was abroad, he'd call his brother, Laz, and ask to be placed on speaker when he knew Sacha was there. He'd flirted and pushed Sacha's buttons, knowing there had to be a reason for the man's explosive reactions. Each phone call seemed to build on whatever was happening between them until Gio's return ignited the powder keg of attraction they had for each other.

"Like I said. Evil." Sacha kissed him, a quick but passionate kiss, before playfully shoving him away, making Gio laugh. He helped Sacha set up the ladder, and then searched for the end of the long, thick garland. Thankfully, the pillar was already equipped to hold each end of the garland that would be wrapped around it.

Sacha climbed up, and Gio handed him the looped metal end. He held the ladder while Sacha tried to secure it. "Damn it. It looks like the hook got bent while in storage. Can you find me a pair of pliers?"

Gio scanned the area and spotted a toolbox on the table across the room. "Sure. Hang on. I'll be right back." He walked to the table and opened the toolbox. There was a pair of pliers right on top. Perfect. Maybe when they got back to the cabin, they could take a nice warm shower together, he could get Sacha on his knees and—

"What the hell is this caught on?"

Gio turned around to see Ace tugging on an

extension cord. What on earth was his friend doing? With a frown, Gio ran his gaze along the cord, following it the length of the floor, where it disappeared behind one of the Christmas trees between a set of pillars. It poked out the other side and continued to.... He gasped.

"Ace, stop!"

His warning came too late.

Ace jerked the extension cord with all his strength, and before Gio could get to the other side of the room, the ladder the cord had been wrapped around toppled to the floor, crashing down with Sacha tangled in it.

CHAPTER TWO

This is not *happening.*

The amount of loud cursing that came out of Joker's mouth was enough to have King swiftly clearing everyone who wasn't family out of the ballroom. Joker would have been grateful if his leg didn't feel like a *steamroller* had driven over it. He lay curled on the floor on his right side, his hands wrapped around his bent left knee because he didn't dare touch the rest of his leg.

"Baby, what's wrong?" Gio asked worriedly as Chip pranced frantically around him, whining and poking his nose into various places, which meant Cookie was the one braced against Joker's back. Duchess...well, Duchess just stood there staring at him, her expression very judgmental, which was about right. She always looked like she had no time for their nonsense.

How the hell had this happened? In all his years of combat as a Green Beret, this kind of thing had never, ever happened to him. Not even during his many years of working in private security had anything like this happened. Because this kind of shit did *not* happen to *him*. He was the most athletic, agile, and fit of all of them.

Gio ran a hand over Joker's hair. "Sweetheart, talk to me."

Joker shook his head, his lips pressed together. He couldn't talk because only more cursing would come out if he opened his mouth.

It's fine. Just breathe through it.

Joker shut his eyes, breathed deeply through his nose, and then let it out through his mouth. When he opened his eyes, Red was there.

Fuck my life.

"Don't say it," Joker gritted through his teeth.

Red's deep frown confirmed what Joker already knew.

"Son of a bitch!"

"What is it?" Gio asked.

"We need to get him to Urgent Care," Red said

gently. "He's fractured his leg." He carefully pulled up Joker's pant leg. "It's already swelling."

"Oh, baby, I'm so sorry."

Why was his boyfriend sorry? He didn't do this. Joker turned his head and narrowed his eyes at Ace, who looked all pouty and worried and pathetic.

"I'm sorry, I should have checked. It was stupid and reckless, and...I'm so sorry."

And now Joker couldn't even be mad because as much of a pain in the ass as his brother was, when Ace was *really* sorry about something he looked like a sad puppy who'd been abandoned out in the cold. Asshole.

"It's fine," Joker said through a grunt as Red took hold of one arm and Gio the other. They helped him up onto his uninjured leg. This was a nightmare, and he wasn't referring to the pain. Pain he could deal with. It was everything else this damn injury was about to unleash that terrified him.

"It's not fine," Ace muttered. "You're hurt, and it's my fault."

"Can we go?" Joker asked. He could feel his leg getting more swollen by the second.

How many members of the Boyfriend Collective did it take to dress Joker for the cold?

All of them.

Oh God, they'd been *activated*. It was too soon. He wasn't prepared.

Mason ran over with his coat, handing it to Colton, who slipped one of Joker's arms into a sleeve while Laz slipped Joker's other arm into the opposite sleeve. Leo wrapped Joker's scarf around him, and Fitz put Joker's hat on him. Oh fuck! This was bad. Very bad. They were going to want to...take care of him. No. Oh no, no, no.

Joker clenched his jaw so he wouldn't tell them all to fuck off and hurt their feelings because each one was like a baby bunny carrying a cinnamon bun surrounded by sunflowers and the glow of the summer sun.

Why the fuck did they all have to be so damned nice? It was the reason he would take down anyone who hurt one of them, but he did *not* need them going into protective-mother-hen mode with *him*.

Thankfully, Gio was there, and he murmured something to Colton, who nodded and corralled the other Boyfriends, ushering them away from Joker. That gave Joker an idea. He could teach Chip to wrangle them. His dog was great at herding!

Fitz somehow escaped and floated over like the Disney princess he was. He threw his arms around Joker's neck and hugged him.

"Don't worry, sweetie. We're going to take good care of you. Whatever you need."

"I need to go to Urgent Care," Joker muttered, his voice muffled by Fitz's fluffy white sweater.

"Oh, sorry! Of course." Fitz turned to Red. "You should carry him to the car."

Red glanced at Joker, who narrowed his eyes.

Don't you fucking dare, Russell.

"I think it's better we not jostle his leg," Red replied.

Nice save.

Fitz nodded and joined the others, leaving Red and Gio to help Joker hop outside. The cold air felt good.

"Do you think they'll knock me out?" Joker asked Red as he helped him into the back of the SUV.

"For a fracture?"

"No, for my sanity."

"Oh." Red shrugged and smiled apologetically. "Sorry, buddy. I don't think so."

Gio climbed into the backseat next to Joker, the dogs jumping in after him. Chip didn't know what to do with himself. He whined and leaned against the seat, his head resting on Joker's thigh. Chip might be expertly trained, but when his person was injured, his best boy fretted. He also stuck to Joker like Velcro, more so than usual.

"How are you holding up, sweetheart?"

"I'll live," Joker grumbled because he'd been through worse. "Fucking hurts, though." Didn't mean he didn't reserve the right to bitch about it.

"My poor Sacha." Gio wrapped his arms around Joker and cradled his head on his shoulder. Joker buried his face in Gio's neck and let out a sigh. This was nice. Mm, his man smelled good. He was one of those guys who everyone loved how he smelled, and he smelled good all the damn time because of some magical combination of moisturizer, subtle cologne, and who the hell knew what else.

Usually, Joker was the one fussing over Gio, making sure he took care of himself, that he hydrated and ate when he should. Gio took better care of himself these days, but that hadn't stopped Joker from looking out for him, making sure Gio wasn't getting up too quickly or showering alone.

Even with Gio's medication, his condition was serious. Joker wasn't fucking around. Gio was the man he loved, and he wouldn't let anything happen to him. Fuck, the pain was making him sappy.

"We're here." Red climbed out, and between him

and Gio, they got Joker inside the Urgent Care building.

Winterhaven was a small town, with the nearest hospital one town over, so their Urgent Care was amazingly equipped. The wait time was also better than any emergency facility he'd ever been to. He'd barely sat down before one of the nurses brought out a wheelchair to take him to radiology. They took X-rays of his leg, wheeled him into one of the curtained-off areas, and helped him get into the pristine hospital bed. They gave him ibuprofen, and Gio was there with him a short time later.

"I'm sorry," Joker muttered.

"For what?"

"They're going to put a cast on, which means getting around is going to be a pain in the ass. This is our Christmas vacation. I wanted you to enjoy it."

"And who says I can't continue to enjoy it?" Gio stood next to Joker's bed and ran his fingers through Joker's hair, knowing how much Joker loved it. "As long as I'm with you, I'm happy. You don't need to worry about that, sweetheart. Let's get you on the road to healing. That's what matters."

Joker let out a low groan.

"Have the painkillers not kicked in yet?" Gio asked.

"I'm groaning because King will give me desk duty when we get back. I *hate* desk duty. Whoever gets desk duty ends up having to do all the paperwork, and paperwork makes me rage-y. Do you have any idea what Ace's paperwork looks like? It's like deciphering a code no one has the key to."

Gio kissed Joker's temple. "We'll worry about that another time."

A few minutes later, the curtains parted, and a tall, dark-haired man in a white coat walked in. He shook Joker's hand. "Mr. Wilder, I'm Dr. Marley." He turned and shook Gio's hand. "Mr. Galanos."

"Hello, doctor," Gio replied. "Thank you for looking after Sacha."

"Yeah, thanks. What's broken?" Joker braced himself. As if he didn't already know what the doctor was going to say.

"I'm afraid you fractured your tibia."

"Great," Joker mumbled.

"The good news is, it's a minor fracture, so no surgery is needed. You'll have to wear a cast for about six weeks."

He supposed it could have been worse. At least it wasn't broken. The doctor showed him his X-rays and explained everything, then walked him through the next steps. When he was done, a couple nurses came in with a bunch of supplies, and before Joker knew it, he had a bright white cast that went from below his knee to just above his toes. They'd also had to cut his pant leg. Gio managed to get Joker's sock over his toes and half his foot, but some larger socks were clearly in order.

A few hours later, Joker was back in the SUV on the way to the cabin with crutches and a walking brace boot. When they got inside the cabin, Red helped him up the stairs to their room with Gio close behind, carrying Joker's newly acquired equipment. Chip and Cookie waited for them at the top of the stairs like good boys. Inside their room, Joker sat on the edge of the bed and sighed in relief.

"You should get some rest," Red said. "I'll check on you later. Is there anything I can get you?"

"No, but there's something you can take with you."

Red smiled knowingly. "I'll let them know that you're napping."

"Thanks." The last thing Joker needed was to have the Boyfriend Collective hovering over him, making a big fuss, except for Gio. He didn't mind if Gio fussed over him. Or ran his fingers through Joker's hair. Or kissed him.

"I know you're going to get tired of hearing this,

but are you sure there's nothing you need?" Gio asked as he helped Joker lay back against the wall of pillows he'd just arranged and fluffed. He covered Joker in a cozy blanket and sat on the edge of the bed where Joker was currently being puppy-eyed by two dogs.

"I'm good," Joker replied through a yawn. Why was he so tired? "Oh wait, there is something." He tapped his lips, and Gio leaned in with a chuckle, kissing him sweetly. It ended way too soon. Joker huffed. "Why are you stopping?"

"Because you need to rest. I'm going downstairs to grab you a water bottle and make you a hot drink."

"Okay." Joker closed his eyes, smiling when Chip snuggled up close, shoving his face under Joker's hand so he could pet him. He let out a little whine, and Joker sighed. "I'm okay, boy." He'd intended on just closing his eyes for a few minutes, but it had clearly been much longer, considering that when he woke up, it was dark outside.

Also, Ace was sitting in the armchair near the bed. Weird.

"How long have you been there?" Joker murmured, side-eyeing his friend.

"You probably don't want me to answer that."

That was wise. "Where's Gio?"

"Downstairs, helping Red make you some chicken and dumpling soup."

Joker's mouth watered. He *loved* Red's chicken and dumpling soup. "That's one of my favorites."

"That's why they're making it."

With a grunt, Joker pushed himself up into a sitting position. Ace jumped to his feet and rushed over.

"I can sit up by myself," Joker warned. "What are you doing here?"

Ace sat on the edge of the bed, looking all pouty. "Are you mad?"

"No." Joker grabbed the remote and turned on the TV. He might as well put on a movie, seeing as he wasn't going anywhere tonight.

"Is that you saying no or the drowsiness saying no?"

"I'm not mad, and I'm not drowsy."

"Because you would tell me if you were, right? Mad, I mean. Not drowsy, though you could tell me that too."

Joker eyed his friend. "When have I not known I was mad at you?"

"True. But this is different. I've never broken your leg before."

For fuck's sake. "You didn't break it. The fall did. And it's not broken. It's a fracture."

"Your bone is no longer solid."

"It's not liquid either."

Ace rolled his eyes. "You know what I mean."

"I'm not mad."

"Really?"

"Really."

Ace opened his mouth, and Joker sighed.

"If you ask me one more time, I will be."

"I still feel bad."

"I'm sure you do, and you should prepare for the day I start rubbing this in your face mercilessly."

Ace winced. "Too soon."

"Go away."

"Will that make you feel better?"

"Yes."

"Okay." Ace stood. "But can I get you anything?"

"More ibuprofen."

"You can't. It's too soon. Can I get you something else?"

"Vodka."

It was Ace's turn to sigh. "Again, painkillers."

"I'm Russian. It's fine."

"I'm just going to go." Ace motioned to the door,

and Joker nodded. He turned his attention back to the TV. A wise decision. Ace left, and Chip lifted his head. He huffed at Joker.

"Why are you sassing *me*? This is *his* fault."

Chip responded with a quiet bark in Ace's defense. Traitor.

"Whatever. He'll get over it. You're supposed to be on *my* side."

The door slowly slid open, and Joker opened his mouth to tell Ace to get lost when a puppy bounded in. Oh, that sneaky bastard. Cocoa darted over to the bed and stood on his hind legs, whining and barking, his tail wagging his entire body and his giant ears irresistible. They were in that wanting-to-stay-up-permanently phase, so one sort of drooped to the side against the other straight one. Puppies were everyone's weakness, but German Shepherd puppies, especially, were Joker's.

"I see how it is. Well played, Sharpe. Well played." Joker leaned over and picked up Cocoa, placing him on his lap. Cocoa crawled up Joker's chest, shoved his little head under Joker's chin, and fell asleep. That sneaky son of a bitch. How dare he make Joker feel all warm and fuzzy!

Maybe this wouldn't be so bad after all. In fact, it

was a good excuse to not get involved in any annoying festivities. He could stay in bed, watching TV and cuddling puppies. He just needed to steal Duchess and he'd have a complete set. Yeah, this was going to be fine.

CHAPTER THREE

"Get back here so I can pummel you!"

Uh oh. Here we go again.

Gio stepped out of the kitchen in time to see Ace round the living room couch, Sacha hopping after him, swinging one of his crutches. Chip ran circles around them, barking, and poor Cookie looked very confused as he watched whatever madness was happening. Good thing the cabin's living room was spacious.

With Ace, three grown dogs, and a puppy, there was no telling what piece of furniture or decorative accent might end up a casualty of their play. Gio's biggest concern was why his boyfriend wore nothing but black boxer briefs.

"I was just trying to help!"

"I didn't ask for your help! I don't need help putting on my pants!"

Ace stopped at the opposite end of the long cream-colored couch and folded his arms over his chest, his smile smug. "Then why did you fall over?"

"Because some asshole came into my room while I was getting dressed and scared the shit out of me," Sacha growled.

"You tripped on your pant leg."

"Because they're Gio's yoga pants, and like the rest of you tall assholes, he's a fucking redwood, so there's a foot of extra fabric!"

A bit of an exaggeration. Depending on who Sacha stood next to, he wasn't *that* much shorter. Okay, maybe there were at least six to seven inches of extra fabric when Sacha wore Gio's pants, but not an extra foot.

"Stop running," Sacha demanded, hopping on his good foot and using his crutch to help him maneuver around the living room.

"So you can hurt me? Um, no."

"Oh, you mean how the floor hurt my body when I collided with it? Because of *you*?"

Ace put his hands up in front of him. "I'll knock next time."

"There will be no next time!"

"Darling," Gio said gently as he walked to Sacha. "Why don't we go back upstairs? I'll finish making your hot chocolate and bring it to you in bed. We could watch a movie."

Sacha narrowed his eyes at Ace. "Babe, I need you to take this crutch and whack him."

"I'm sure Ace meant well."

"See?" Ace said. "Not my fault. You're just being grumpy, and I understand. You have every right to be a grumpy pants. Speaking of pants, you might want to put some on. Just saying."

Sacha lunged at Ace, but Gio threw his arms around him, catching him before he could fall. Again. Sacha tried to hit Ace with his crutch, but considering how far away Ace stood, he was mainly swinging at the air. The front door opened, and everyone flooded in, stopping inside to stare at them. They must've made quite the picture. Not that any of their family would be at all surprised by this situation.

"I don't want to know," King grumbled, heading for the kitchen.

Sacha thrust his crutch in Ace's direction. "It's *his* fault."

"I'm sure it is," King said as he walked to the

fridge, not in the least bit fazed by whatever was happening.

"Ouch." Ace put a hand to his heart.

"Did Ace steal your clothes?" Leo asked. He frowned at Ace. "Why would you steal his clothes? He's injured."

"I didn't steal his clothes. He fell out of them. Wait, that didn't come out right." Ace shook his head, then burst into laughter.

"What's so funny?" Sacha demanded.

Ace pointed behind them, and they turned to see Chip with his left paw up as he hopped across the room. Then he flopped to the floor and rolled over, paws up.

"Are you sassing me?" Sacha turned back to Ace. "You put him up to this."

"I did not. But I kinda wish I had. There was more flailing when you did it, though."

"I'm gonna murder you!"

"Okay. You leave me no choice," Gio said, lifting Sacha to carry him over his shoulder.

Sacha gasped. "What are you doing? Don't use your fine body against me. Put me down!"

"I think he needs a nap," Ace whispered loud enough for everyone to hear.

"Colton, I hope his insurance policy is up to date

because I'm about to murder your husband. Leo, find me the perfect place to hide the body. Fitz, get the shovels. Mason, keep the law away. Chip, do something!"

Glancing over his shoulder, the only thing Chip did was drown Ace in doggy kisses. Gio told Chip and Cookie to stay with Uncle Colton. Gio had plans for his grumpy, half-naked sweetheart. It was still early. Not even lunchtime. Though it would explain why Sacha had been getting dressed. Where exactly had he been going?

"Everyone's against me," Sacha grumbled as Gio carried him upstairs. When they reached the bedroom, he put Sacha on his feet and closed the door behind them. He locked it and turned, holding back a smile at his pouty boyfriend. Gio couldn't take it.

"Come here." He slid his arms around Sacha and pulled him close. "Why are you so damned cute?"

Sacha narrowed his eyes at him. "I'm sorry, what did you call me?"

"Gorgeous? Beautiful? Stunning?"

"Better." Sacha wrinkled his nose. "I'll *think* about forgiving you. No promises. You sided with the annoying one."

It took a lot for Gio not to laugh. "I'm sorry." He

lowered his head and kissed Sacha, cupping the back of his head. Damn, but he tasted good. Gio couldn't seem to get enough of him. "Why don't you get into bed and rest."

"I rested last night and most of today. I'm rested out."

It was not a surprise that Sacha had gotten over resting in bed in such a short amount of time. Most people would appreciate getting to relax and have someone take care of them. Not Sacha. When he was sick or injured, he took it as an insult to his very being. Much of the time, he refused even to believe he was ill. The idea that a common cold could defeat him was laughable. In this instance, Gio needed his sweetheart to rest and stay off his leg.

"What if I help you relax?"

Sacha sighed. "I can't get on my knees."

The words made Gio groan. There was something about seeing Sacha on his knees that made Gio painfully hard. He carefully walked Sacha back to the bed, his mouth on the soft skin of Sacha's neck. "What do you want?" he asked, his voice low. "What can I do for you? Or better yet, *to* you."

Sacha lifted his face and nipped at Gio's chin. He turned and bent over the side of the bed, his legs spread. The black boxer briefs stretched over his beautifully rounded ass like a second skin.

The look Sacha gave Gio over his shoulder was sinful, sending a shiver through Gio and making him groan. There was nothing more erotic than Sacha submitting to him.

Gio stepped in between Sacha's legs and brushed his fingers down his spine, loving the way Sacha moaned. Sacha was beautiful, from his athletic dancer's body— shoulders tapering to a slender waist and defined muscles beneath smooth fair skin—to his fierce, loyal, and passionate heart. This was a man who had spent his life raging some kind of war and had only recently found his peace, and Gio was blessed to have been a part of that.

Opening the nightstand drawer, Gio removed the bottle of lube. He tossed it onto the bed and then helped Sacha remove his boxer briefs, flinging them to one side. Getting down on his knees, Gio spread Sacha's legs and ran his hands up his thighs to his ass. He spread his cheeks and used his tongue to have his incredible man writhing and trembling with need. Gio cherished this man, loved him deep to his core, and he needed Sacha to know it each and every time Gio made love to him.

"Oh, fuck. Baby, please." Sacha arched his back,

his fingers flexing as he grabbed fistfuls of the blanket. He dropped his brow onto the mattress, his breath panting.

As much as Gio wanted to continue tasting Sacha and driving him wild with his tongue, he was more desperate to be inside his gorgeous ass. Gio lubed his fingers and leaned over Sacha, his chest pressed to Sacha's back. The fact Gio was still dressed was not lost on Sacha, and he let out a low, deep moan. His man did not like to feel vulnerable, except when he was naked under Gio. Then he gave himself over completely.

Gio pushed one finger inside Sacha, groaning at Sacha's sharp intake of breath. As much as he wanted to take his time, he wanted to be inside Sacha, so he quickly but carefully prepped him, first with one finger, then two, until it looked like Sacha might come apart.

"Fuck, Gio. Come on. I need you...."

Gio nipped at Sacha's ear. "I love that you need me."

"Always," Sacha murmured, breathless. "You... you mean the world to me, Giovanni."

With a groan, Gio stood and added a generous amount of lube to his cock. He lined himself up and carefully pushed inside, his fingers digging into

Sacha's shoulder. He gritted his teeth at the delicious tight heat as he pushed himself inside the man he loved. When he'd buried himself completely, he paused, his groin against Sacha's ass. Confident he wouldn't come just yet, he started moving slowly. Each gasp and curse Sacha released pushed Gio closer to the edge.

Taking hold of Sacha's slender waist, Gio drove himself inside Sacha over and over, his brow beaded with sweat as he fucked his boyfriend. The bed moved beneath them, the sound of their panting breaths filling the room. Feeling like his skin was on fire, Gio quickly unbuttoned his shirt and tugged it off, letting it fall to the floor. Sacha looked at him over his shoulder.

"You okay?"

Gio nodded. He was a little breathless but it was nothing to worry about. He pressed his naked chest to Sacha's back and kissed him, their mouths wet and greedy. They kissed as Gio pumped himself inside Sacha, his orgasm building and rolling through him.

"Baby," Gio breathed.

"Come inside me," Sacha pleaded, and Gio didn't need to be told twice. He fucked Sacha deep and hard, chasing the white light of his orgasm until it exploded, and he growled Sacha's name as he came hard. As much as he wanted to lay there, he wanted to give Sacha more pleasure. He pulled out, straightened, and turned Sacha around.

Getting on his knees, he brought Sacha's hard, leaking cock into his mouth and sucked. The feel of Sacha's fingers threaded tightly through his hair made him moan. The more he was given, the more he wanted. When it came to Sacha, Gio was insatiable, and he loved it.

Sacha cried out and came inside his mouth. He shivered, and Gio carefully pulled off, though he stayed on his knees, resting his head on Sacha's thigh, and enjoying the tender and intimate way Sacha stroked his hair. As incredible as the sex was, *these* were the moments Gio lived for, when all of Sacha's defenses were down.

"Hey," Sacha said gently, and Gio lifted his head. He smiled at Sacha, whose plump lips were pink and wet from their kissing. They tugged up at the corner, his beautiful face flushed. The adoration in those big blue-gray eyes stole Gio's breath away every time. "I'm happy you're here with me."

Gio blinked at him. Those kinds of admissions were rare. He slid his hands up and around Sacha's thighs, wrapping Sacha in his arms. With a happy heart, Gio let his head rest against Sacha's stomach. He closed his eyes and let out a happy sigh.

"There is nowhere else I would rather be," Gio replied. "And no one else I would rather be with."

"I know I can be difficult—"

Gio stood and cupped Sacha's face. "I fell in love with you just as you are. That will never change."

"You're weird."

Gio laughed softly. He brushed his lips over Sacha's, his kiss feathery soft. "Must be what makes us perfect for each other."

"Hm, must be." Sacha smiled. "Now, find me some pants."

Gio cocked his head and tapped a finger to his lips. "I didn't bring any shorts."

"Oh, you fuck," Sacha laughed. He snatched a pillow off the bed and smacked Gio with it, making him laugh. The fact that Gio was the only one who could tease Sacha about his height made his heart flip. It wasn't that Sacha was self-conscious about his height. He was just annoyed that the rest of the men in his family were taller.

"I'm kidding," Gio said. He popped a kiss on Sacha's lips. "I'll get you some clothes." Or rather, he knew who he'd ask to get Sacha some clothes. "Now get into bed."

"Help me put on my underwear. The second you unlock that door, someone will hear it and appear. It's like they have sonar or something."

Gio chuckled and leaned over to pick up Sacha's boxer briefs off the floor.

"Easy," Sacha warned him, and Gio smiled softly. His boyfriend was always looking out for him. Gio made sure not to get up too fast so he wouldn't make himself dizzy.

Over the past almost two years, Gio had grown accustomed to living with mild autonomic neuropathy. The symptoms varied depending on the severity of the condition. For Gio, it messed with his heart rate and blood pressure. The medication made a huge difference, and he no longer passed out like he used to, but that didn't mean he could go back to living the way he had been before his diagnosis. He remembered that day quite clearly. Sacha had been furious with him, and rightfully so.

Gio had been foolish for so long, refusing to believe there'd been anything wrong with his health when, in fact, he'd been walking around with a life-threatening condition. He'd lost count of how many times he'd passed out.

Sacha had called him out on his bullshit and made him see the truth. Gio's life had changed. He wasn't the same man he'd been before the terrifying ordeal of his kidnapping or the infection that came after that almost killed him and left him with a compromised nervous system. When he got lost in his work, as he tended to do at times, Cookie reminded him of his promise to Sacha that he'd take better care of himself.

"You look like there's a lot of thinking going on in your brain," Sacha said from his position on the bed. He looked beautiful and tantalizing, sitting back against the many pillows, naked, his knee drawn up on his good leg. Gio walked to the bed and helped him into his boxer briefs before unlocking the door and returning to sit on the edge of the bed next to Sacha.

"Just thinking about when I was in the hospital. How mad you were when the doctor told you about my condition."

Sacha arched a thick eyebrow at him. "You mean when you were being an ass and I wanted to strangle you? Yeah, I remember very clearly."

"I hate to think where I would be if you hadn't been there to knock some sense into me or if I hadn't come home at all."

Sacha frowned, his brows drawn together. "I'd rather not think about that." He took Gio's hand in his and laced their fingers together. "What matters is that you're here and you listened to me. Because I'm always right."

Gio barked out a laugh. "Oh, really?"

"Yep."

"Not just a pretty face then?"

"That's right. Now get over here and kiss this pretty face."

Gio leaned in and happily obliged. He hummed against Sacha's lips until a scratch at the door made Gio chuckle. No need to guess who that was, Chip had barely let Sacha out of his sight since they got home from Urgent Care.

Sacha shook his head. "Better let him in before he knocks down the door. Or worse, brings Ace."

"He feels bad about what happened," Gio said, letting in Chip and Cookie. They rushed to the bed and hopped up, licking Sacha like they hadn't seen him in years before settling next to him.

"I know he does. But it's Ace. His trying to fix things will only lead to him breaking something, and that something will be me. Oh, wait."

Gio shook his head, amused. "He's just trying to help." He pulled one of Sacha's T-shirts from the dresser drawer, and when he turned around, he had the life scared out of him.

"Holy shit!" Gio put a hand to his chest. "Ace, for the love of—Why are you sneaking up on me?" His friend knew better. Anything that shot his heart rate up suddenly was not good.

Ace frowned. "I just walked into the room."

Gio looked to Sacha and narrowed his gaze. "Really? You couldn't have warned me?"

"I saw him when you did," Sacha replied, throwing his arms up. "I keep saying we need to put a bell on him, but no one listens."

"I'm not a cat," Ace grumbled. He cocked his head. "Though a bell would be incredibly annoying, so maybe not such a bad idea. I could get one of those jester hats with all the dangly bells."

"No," Gio said, shaking his head. He threw Sacha's T-shirt at him, hitting him in the face and making him laugh.

"But 'he's just trying to help'," Sacha repeated Gio's earlier words back to him, his grin smug. "How's that working out for you?"

CHAPTER FOUR

This sucked.

Joker sipped his eggnog and wrinkled his nose. Ugh, there was no booze in this. Discreetly, he glanced around and saw that his family was busy mingling or doing whatever they did during a holiday party. With a flick of his wrist, he tossed his cup into the trash bin next to the table. Turning, he poured himself some eggnog from the spiked eggnog punch bowl. He lifted the cup to his lips, only to have Fitz pluck it from his hand. *Son of a—*

"Hey!" Where the hell had he even come from?

"Nope," Fitz said, stopping long enough to kiss his cheek before floating off, taking Joker's spiked eggnog with him.

Damn it! His family was trying to kill him. How

did they expect him to make it through the holidays in this terrifyingly cheerful town without the ability to escape or drink alcohol? Why did his family have to be so annoying, looking out for his freaking well-being all the time? It was exhausting.

King stepped up to him, and Joker sighed.

"What?"

"You should be sitting."

"And you should be figuring out what your boyfriend is up to."

King arched an eyebrow at him and pointed to Joker's empty chair at their table. "Sit."

"Oh yeah?" Joker lifted his chin defiantly. "And what if I don't?"

"I will pick you up and put you there."

Damn. He would too.

"Fine," Joker growled and used his crutches to help him get to the table because Red insisted he not put weight on his leg, and if he did, one of his jerk brothers would tell on him. *Snitches get stitches, assholes.* With a huff, he dropped into the empty chair and rested his crutches against the chair next to him. Stupid party. He'd wanted to stay home, but Gio said getting out of the cabin would be good for him. Whatever.

Decorating was finally complete, and to

celebrate, the town was hosting a big party in the main ballroom. The place was packed with townspeople and the volunteers staying at the lodge. Naturally, everyone wanted to talk to Gio.

From the moment they'd stepped foot in the Ice Castle, Gio had been swarmed by people, which was nothing new. Sacha didn't care about all the attention his boyfriend got during parties. Gio was tall, elegant, and gorgeous, with a dazzling smile and an amazing heart. Everything he did to help people, to help pair veterans with service dogs through his charity, made Joker incredibly proud of him.

When they'd first started dating, they'd agreed that Joker didn't need to be for Gio what Ace was for Colton. Gio didn't need Joker to stand at his side while he worked the room.

Ace was Colton's biggest supporter, and although Joker was there for Gio should his boyfriend need him, Ace was as social, if not more so, than Colton. He loved talking to people, telling ridiculous stories, and entertaining people. He always knew what to say and how to move the attention away from Colton when Colton started feeling overwhelmed.

The difference between Colton and Gio? Colton eventually got tired of peopling, whereas Gio was energized by it. There was a reason Gio helped people, and Joker worked with dogs. People didn't just exhaust him, they annoyed him. Right now, one person in particular was annoying him, and he hated it because he was *not* that guy.

"Are you trying to set her on fire with your mind?" Fitz asked quietly from the seat next to Joker.

Joker gave a start. "For fuck's sake. Are you taking lessons from Ace? Where did you come from?"

"Maybe if you weren't so focused on trying to make Mariam spontaneously combust, you would have noticed me," Fitz said sweetly.

"I don't know what you're talking about," Joker grumbled.

"Right. Your constant attempt to spike your drinks has nothing to do with Gio's ex-girlfriend being here swooning all over him."

Joker glared at Fitz but didn't reply. Man, he could use a drink. He was not intimidated by the stunning woman with killer curves and wavy dark hair cascading over her shoulders who was also fucking *taller* than him, and she wasn't even wearing heels.

Mariam was not a surprise. Gio told Joker about her back when they'd first started dating. Mariam and Gio had hooked up years ago during a London charity gala. They'd dated for almost a year, but Gio's schedule had been intense at the time, so when she realized she was falling for him and that he had no intention of slowing down anytime soon, she walked away before he could break her heart. They'd remained friends, and she spent most of her time abroad, so Joker hadn't given her another thought. But Mariam was no longer abroad.

Joker understood it. He did. Gio's schedule had been a source of many of their arguments when they'd first gotten together, but Gio didn't have that schedule anymore, and Mariam was back. *That* was why Joker was grumpy. Gio was the one who got away, and the fact Gio had a boyfriend didn't stop her from flirting and *touching* him. Of course, Gio was such a nice fucking guy that it didn't even cross his mind that someone would try to lure him away from his boyfriend.

"I thought charity people were supposed to be fucking saints," Joker growled as Mariam laughed at something Gio said and playfully smacked his arm. He was pretty sure whatever Gio had said wasn't *that* funny.

"I don't think I've ever seen you jealous," Fitz said with a hum.

"I'm not jealous. I'm...concerned."

Fitz pulled his chair closer and petted Joker's arm. "Oh, sweetie. She's got nothing on you. Besides, you know Gio adores you. He was smitten with you before you two even met in person." He took one of the gingerbread cookies off the plate on the table. It had frosted hair and a skirt. He snapped the head off and handed it to Joker, who couldn't help but smirk as he took it and popped it into his mouth. He was in good company.

"They traveled the world together doing good. The only reason it didn't work out was because of Gio's schedule."

"A schedule that no longer exists," Fitz said, nodding his understanding. "And what do you think Gio is going to do?"

"Nothing." Joker trusted Gio completely. That wasn't even up for debate. His concern was one he'd been trying to ignore for months now. "What if she reminds him of everything he gave up? When we started dating, he told me he'd been thinking of coming home anyway, that he'd been missing Laz and having a family, but he spent *decades* traveling the world doing his thing. It hasn't even been three years since he got back. What if...what if he realizes he made a mistake?"

"Has he told you he misses it?"

"No, but that doesn't mean he doesn't. If Gio ends up resenting me, it'll crush me." He frowned down at his fingers. "I really love him, Fitz. I...I could see us...you know."

"No, I don't."

Joker glared at his friend. "You're going to make me say it, aren't you?"

Fitz blinked innocently at him. "I don't know what you mean."

"Asshole. Fine. I could see us married. Okay? Happy? I can see us having the whole happy ever after with the salmon pink house, white picket fence, and two furry kids."

Fitz squeaked and clapped his hands together. "I knew that's why you ran that night after you saw the rings."

Joker opened his mouth to deny it, but Fitz crossed his arms over his chest, that perfectly shaped brow arched high.

"Yeah, fine. That's why I ran."

"I knew it!" Fitz let out a dreamy sigh. "Honey, you two were meant to be. I know these things." He motioned behind him, and Joker spotted the result of Fitz's meddling matchmaking on the other side of the room. Merry and Noel were ridiculously sweet. Noel held out a plate of treats, and when Merry reached for them, Noel stole a kiss. Joker could see Merry's blush from here.

"Merry is like the exact opposite of me," Joker said. The young man was so damned cheerful and excitable.

"You're not that different." Mischief filled Fitz's eyes, and Joker braced himself. "You're both adorable and fun-sized."

"I will beat you with my crutch," Joker growled.

Fitz laughed. He threw his arms around Joker's neck. "You're a grump, and I love you."

"Yeah, yeah. I love you too. Even if you are a pain in my ass."

A kiss to his cheek, and Fitz stood. "I need to go. My boyfriend is arguing with our diva again, and you know what happens when she doesn't get her way."

Joker snickered. He did know. She stomped her furry paws and threw a temper tantrum that included howling, barking, singing the song of her people, and then running off with something.

"If you're worried, tell him," Fitz said gently. "This is Gio we're talking about."

Fitz was right. Joker was probably reading too much into it anyway. He was feeling grumpy and crappy from his cast, which was heavy, uncomfortable, and had entered the itching-the-shit-out-of-him phase. He knew better than to stick anything in there, but fuck, it was driving him nuts, and he couldn't exactly walk around with a hair dryer to blow cold air into it. Yep, he was just being a miserable fuck.

Maybe he could bribe one of the Boyfriends into bringing him some spiked eggnog or cider, or hell, he'd even take an Irish coffee. Laz and Red had stayed home with Cocoa and Chip. Red hadn't been feeling a crowded ballroom tonight, and Laz was always happy to hang back with his boyfriend. Not that Red would have let Joker drink, and seeing as how Laz was Gio's brother, he'd have been out of the question anyway. Leo was with King, so he was out. Colton was Gio's best friend, so that was a bust. Damn it. Oh! Mason!

Joker shot Mason a text, and a heartbeat later, the cowboy strolled over to the table.

"Hey, everything okay?"

"My cast is itching like fuck. I need you to do me a favor."

Mason peered at him. "If it's booze, you can forget about it. We've all been warned. I love you, man, but I ain't about to piss off Red."

Joker scowled at him. "Since when are you scared of Red, Cowboy?"

Mason snorted. "Oh, I ain't scared of Red, but I sure am scared of losing out on his Christmas dinner. No one's coming between me and Red's onion casserole."

"You're putting onion casserole over my needs?"

Mason blinked at him. "Why yes, yes I am. Now, is there anything I can get you that is not alcohol?"

"No," Joker grumbled. He waved Mason off. "Go back to sucking face with your annoying boyfriend who also won't get me alcohol."

Mason chuckled and walked away. Joker was about to search out his own booze again when someone sat beside him.

Mariam.

"Hi! Sacha, right?" Her red-lipped smile was wide as she put her hair up in a messy bun, her cropped, slinky red sweater rising to reveal her bronzed skin and flat stomach.

Joker managed to paste on a smile. "Everyone calls me Joker."

"Except Gio," she chirped.

"Except Gio."

"This place is amazing. I'm so glad I got back in

time to be here. I almost missed spending Christmas with Gio in this beautiful town."

Joker straightened. "Spending Christmas with Gio?"

Mariam waved a hand. "You know what I mean. Spending Christmas in Winterhaven."

Why would Joker know what she meant? He didn't know *her*.

"Thank you for letting me borrow Gio tomorrow."

Joker hummed as he took a sip of his water, pretending he knew what the fuck she was talking about. Borrow Gio for what?

"He wanted you to come with us, but with all the walking around in the snow we'll be doing, I told him that might not be such a great idea."

I bet.

"I mean, walking with crutches is challenging enough without adding ice to the mix. We wouldn't want you to hurt yourself again."

Joker stared at her. Hurt himself? He hadn't hurt himself. The ladder being pulled out from under him had hurt him.

"Besides, it's just for a few hours. He's been stuck in the cabin for days taking care of you. He could use a little break." She batted her long, mascaraed lashes. "He's so attentive and nurturing. I've always loved that about him."

Stuck in the cabin taking care of him? What the fuck? There was *no way* Gio had used those words. If she was looking to get a reaction out of him, she was about to get one. He opened his mouth when a child appeared next to him. Well, fuck.

"I better get back to Gio. He's waiting for me. See you, Sacha." Mariam jumped to her feet and pranced off to Gio, her moves causing her breasts to bounce. Joker could appreciate a beautiful woman. He'd had plenty in his bed over the years, had even become friends with some of them, but this one? This one, he wanted to push in front of a moving sleigh.

"Why are you sad?" Dotty asked. "I brought you a cookie because you looked sad." She handed him a dog-shaped sugar cookie with a red bow on its neck.

Joker smiled. "Thanks, Dotty. I like your dress."

Dotty looked down at her red plaid and green velvet dress, then whirled around. "Thank you! I picked it out myself."

"I'm not surprised. You're very stylish. The lights on the tiara are a nice touch."

"I told Mommy that it needed lights. How else would people know it's a Christmas tiara?"

"A sound argument," Joker replied with a nod.

Dotty cocked her head to one side and then looked out at the floor. "Are you sad because that lady is making kissy faces at your boyfriend?"

Joker turned his head, his hackles rising at Mariam, who was very obviously pouting her lips at Gio. And his boyfriend? Fucking *oblivious*. Turning back to Dotty, he barked out a laugh. She'd sucked in her cheeks, making fish lips and kissing noises, her hands on her hips.

"That's exactly what she looks like," Joker said. "You need to pretend you're flipping your hair back, though." He demonstrated, and Dotty expertly did the same with one of her pigtails, then giggled.

"Is she trying to steal your boyfriend? Is she a hussy? She doesn't look like a hussy."

Joker almost choked on his saliva. "Um...what?"

"I like hussies. They're so pretty, and they love the snow! I asked Mommy if we could get a hussy, and she looked very confused, too, like you. But then I heard Miss Rita telling Miss Bernadette that only hussies steal boyfriends. I don't want a hussy if they're going to steal my Mommy's boyfriend. That's just not done."

Joker could barely contain himself. She was *adorable*. He put a fist to his mouth, and when he knew he wouldn't fall out of his chair laughing, he responded. "Dotty. What you're thinking of is a *husky*. It's a type of dog. You were talking about a dog, right? Fluffy tail, pointy ears, usually have blue eyes, talk a lot?"

"Well, yes, obviously."

"Obviously."

Dotty's little brows drew together, and she planted her fists on her hips. "So what's a hussy then?"

"Oh, sweetie, that's a question for your Mommy."

Speaking of....

Amara appeared, her smile bright as she greeted him. "And what are you two giggling about over here?"

Dotty looked up at her mother. "Mommy, I was confused. What I want is a *husky*, not a hussy. What's a hussy? Is she a hussy?" Dotty pointed behind them, and they turned to find Gio and Mariam standing there, gaping at them.

Amara gasped. "Oh sweet Jesus. I'm so sorry. She's confused. We're going to go now." She quickly ushered Dotty away.

"But Mommy, I think she's a hussy trying to steal Sacha's boyfriend! That's just not done!"

Joker covered his mouth with his hand. Ever since Dotty heard Gio call him Sacha, she called him that, too. He didn't mind. She was so damned cute. He glanced over at Gio, whose mouth hung open. Seeming to snap himself out of it, he finally closed his mouth and turned to Joker. He looked confused. Mariam looked pissed, not that Joker gave a fuck.

Joker shrugged. "Kids. Aren't they just precious?"

"Are you telling people I'm a hussy?" Mariam demanded.

"What?" Joker frowned. "No. Dotty was the one who said it. Not me."

Mariam folded her arms over her chest. "That child is six years old at most. She doesn't know what a hussy is."

"Exactly. She thought it was a dog," Joker said, but that just seemed to make Miriam even angrier. "I'm not calling you a dog. Dotty had confused husky with hussy. You know what, I don't need to explain myself to you."

"Sacha, what's going on?" Gio asked.

Mariam wrapped her arms around Gio's, her eyes glassy. "I can't believe your boyfriend called me that. Is that what he's been telling people? That I'm some kind of home-wrecker?"

"I'm sure that's not—" Gio stopped when Joker said nothing. "Sacha?"

"Really?" Joker shook his head. "Unbelievable." Then he saw them. Really saw them. They looked so fucking beautiful together.

Joker stood, grabbed his coat off the back of his chair, shoved it on, grabbed his crutches, and headed for the door. His painkillers were starting to wear off, his leg was itching like fuck, and if he stayed, he was going to say something he'd regret.

With his heart hurting, he went out into the cold, though he didn't feel the bitter wind. He told himself it was the falling snow making his cheeks wet. Ugh, it was just his injury making him feel like this. He needed some air, that was all.

CHAPTER FIVE

What just happened?

Gio grabbed his coat off the chair and quickly put it on when Mariam stopped him.

"Don't go. Stay here. With me."

"What?" Gio stared at her. "Mariam, I need to go after him. Something's wrong."

"I'm sure he's fine." Mariam slipped her arm around his waist and pouted. "Wouldn't you rather stay here?"

"What are you doing?" Gio took a quick step back. "Mariam, I'm sorry if I've done something to make you think I'm interested in anything other than friendship. I'm in a relationship."

"He's cute, Gio, but he's not right for you."

"*Excuse me?*"

"Your bodyguard? What were you thinking? After everything that happened?"

A chill went through Gio. Had he heard right? What the hell was happening right now? "Are you... are you seriously comparing Sacha to the bastard who helped kidnap me?" His blood boiled. He needed to go.

She seemed to realize her mistake. Her face flushed as she squeezed his arm. "No, of course not. I'm sorry. I just meant that we were so good together, Gio. Walking away from you was the biggest mistake of my life. I want to be with you."

"What? Mariam, I'm with someone else, and you don't seem to care."

"Just think about it. We could travel the world together just like before. Now that your schedule isn't crazy, we could actually spend time together."

"The only person I want to spend time with is the one who needs me right now." Gio removed her hand from his arm. How had he not seen it? "You're not the person I thought you were, Mariam. I am deeply in love with Sacha. He means more to me than anything, and if you can't accept that, then I'm afraid there's no place for you in my life. Excuse me."

She nodded and quietly walked away. Gio zipped his coat up and told Cookie to find Uncle

Colton. Ignoring the concerned looks from his family, he ran out of the ballroom.

"Sacha?" he called out.

Maybe Sacha was still somewhere in the Ice Castle? His gut told him he wouldn't be. Sacha was angry and hurt. He would want to get as far away as possible. Damn it! Gio was so angry with himself. How had he not known? Again, he'd been so wrapped up in his job that he hadn't realized something was wrong with the man he wanted to spend the rest of his life with.

Outside, it was snowing, making the night appear more beautiful and, at the same time, lonely. The main street was silent, with everyone at the party or in the market square. Gio removed his phone and called Sacha. There was no answer, so he hung up and sent Sacha a text asking him where he was. Nothing.

Not waiting for a response, Gio started walking. There weren't many places where Sacha could be. Their family was back at the party, and the SUVs were still parked on the street.

Most of the shops were closed at this time of night. He doubted Sacha would have gone to the ice skating rink or the busy market. Gio sent a couple more texts before checking the pub, just in case, but the owner, Clarence, hadn't seen Sacha come in.

Time passed, and Gio hadn't received a response to any of his texts. Where could Sacha be? If his boyfriend wanted to be alone somewhere, where would he go? Somewhere he could sit. Gio remembered the small children's park behind the town. They'd gone there just this morning with the dogs.

Gio was a little breathless, but he put it down to walking around in the cold. The snow was really coming down now, and the wind had picked up. Thankfully, he made it to the park just as a dizzy spell hit him. His heart rate had picked up from the stress, and he knew why. He was so fucking scared. What if he'd messed things up with Sacha? He'd worked himself up and needed to calm down, take one of his pills.

Sitting on the first bench he spotted inside the park, he reached into his pocket. With a frown, he checked the other one. Shit. Where were his pills? Wait. This was his black coat. *Damn it*. He'd switched coats this morning and, in helping Sacha get the dogs ready for the park, Gio forgot to take the spare bottle of pills out of his other coat. He closed his eyes and breathed, using the technique his therapist had taught him.

How the hell had this happened? He lay on the bench, afraid he might pass out. Removing his phone, he sent one more text to Sacha. The same one he'd sent back when they'd first started dating, the first time he'd done something foolish and feared he'd lost Sacha.

I need you.

Closing his eyes, he was grateful for the awning over the bench. He was cold, but at least he wasn't wet. An empty park bench in the middle of winter wasn't an ideal place for him to pass out, but he really didn't have a choice.

"What are you doing?"

Gio opened his eyes at that beautiful, growly voice. "I left my pills in my other coat."

"Good thing I always have some on me."

"You do?"

Sacha nodded and removed a little pill bag from his coat pocket. "There's a water fountain over there. Do you think you're okay to get up?"

With a nod, Gio carefully sat up. He was dizzy but okay. He pulled off one of his gloves, took the pill bag from Sacha, removed one, and got up to get a sip of water. Pill down, he returned to Sacha.

"How long have you been carrying spare pills?" Gio asked, warmth spreading through him at the thoughtfulness. But then, that was Sacha, always thinking of Gio.

"Since we started dating. Why did you need your medication?" Sacha asked as he sat on the bench.

Gio sat next to him. "Because I got myself worked up, and I got scared."

"Of what?"

"That I had messed things up with you." Gio sighed. "I'm so sorry. I should have seen what was happening. She asked me about the Echo K9 Foundation, and I got so wrapped up in telling her about it that I was completely clueless about her intentions. I thought we were friends, and she thought there was an opportunity for more."

"I knew it!" Sacha got up and grabbed his crutches. He started pacing, or at least did his best to, considering his cast. "When I saw her with her hands on you, I was like, 'Fuck, they make such a beautiful couple. Maybe he's better off with her,' and then I was sitting on that swing over there, and a fucking squirrel of all things—don't tell Ace— jumped from the branch it was on, causing a fucking avalanche of snow to fall on my head, and it hit me. I mean, the snow literally hit me, obviously, but it also hit me that I was a being a fucking asshole. The fuck I was going to let someone take the man I love from me. I don't think so. I was Special Forces. A fucking Green Beret. I will *end* her. If she thinks a bounce of her perky boobs is going to be enough to get you to leave *me*, oh, she has no idea."

Sacha turned and waved a crutch. "I might be a grumpy asshole who curses a hell of a lot, leaves his shit everywhere, and sheds almost as much as his dog, but I dare anyone to tell me they can fucking love you as much as I do. Okay, so I could do better in the romance department, but that doesn't mean you're not my whole fucking world. I might not spout poems and shit, but sometimes I wake up in the middle of the night and see you there and think of how I'm the luckiest bastard in the world. I'm shit at giving gifts, but that doesn't stop me from getting breathless every time you smile at me. You're gorgeous and smart, and the kindest and most generous person I know, and you smell so fucking good all the time. You make me so happy it hurts, and fuck anyone who thinks they can take that from me."

Gio bit down on his bottom lip, his vision blurry from the tears he was holding back. At the silence, Sacha turned, his eyes going wide.

"Why are you crying? Oh my god, is it that bad? I'll try harder, Gio. I promise. I love you so fucking much."

Gio stood and closed the short distance between them. He cupped Sacha's face and kissed him so deeply and thoroughly that there was no way Sacha could think Gio would *ever* love anyone else the way he loved Sacha. Pulling back, he couldn't help his smile at the dazed look on Sacha's face.

"My beautiful Sacha. I am yours, heart, body, and soul." He kissed Sacha again, holding him close. When they pulled back, Sacha let his head fall against Gio's chest.

"I'm sorry I was such a grump. I...got scared, too."

"Of Mariam?"

Sacha shook his head. "That one of these days, you'll wake up and remember everything you gave up, that you were happier traveling the world. You have to miss it, Gio. You'd been traveling since you graduated college, and since you've been back, you've only been to a handful of places."

"I won't lie. Sometimes, I do miss it," Gio admitted.

Sacha nodded but didn't look up.

It amazed Gio how his man could be so fearless

and strong, capable of charging into battle, and at the same time, be so vulnerable and timid that he was afraid to look Gio in the eye, afraid of what he might find.

Gio ran his fingers through Sacha's hair. "I loved that I got the chance to travel to all those amazing places, but it's different now because when I think about everywhere I visited, I think about how much better it would have been if you'd been there with me."

Sacha's head shot up, blue-gray eyes wide. "Really?"

"Yes. I think about all the things I would have shown you. How much fun we would have had, all the nights making love, all the laughter."

"I...had no idea."

"Guess we're still learning to communicate with each other."

"I guess."

"Besides, nothing says we can't travel together." Gio took Sacha's hand and brought it to his heart. "All you have to do is say the word, and we'll be on a plane to wherever you want to go, you know that. I've offered many times."

Sacha blinked. "Well, shit."

"What?"

"I get it now."

Gio was puzzled. "Get what?"

"Ace. I always wondered how he could be okay with Colton spending money on him all the time, but it's not about the money. Whenever you brought up taking the jet somewhere, I thought it was just you wanting to spend money on me, and because I couldn't accept that and I couldn't afford to pay my own way, I turned you down. But that's not what it was at all." Sacha met his gaze. "You offer to pay because you can, but it has nothing to do with money and everything to do with us building a life together, making memories, having experiences."

Gio smiled warmly. "Sacha, whether we're standing in the middle of a small town park in Winterhaven or the Colosseum in Rome, what matters is that you're with me. My wealth simply affords me the opportunity to show you the world. *If* it's something you want."

"Maybe..." Sacha seemed to think about it. "Maybe when we get back, we can look at our schedules and start making some plans?"

"Nothing would make me happier," Gio said, his heart filled with so much joy he could barely contain it. The possibilities excited him. There were so many places he wanted to show Sacha. "Right now, though, I think the only place we need to go is indoors where it's warm. I can call someone to give us a ride back to the cabin."

Sacha surprised Gio by shaking his head. "Let's go back to the party."

"Really?"

"Yep. I'm here to celebrate the holidays with the man I love, so let's go celebrate."

Gio kissed Sacha. "I'd like that."

They headed back to the Ice Castle, and inside Gio took both their coats, placing them on the back of their chairs at their table. Cookie came running over, tail wagging happily. Gio gave him love and told him he was a good boy. With a happy smile, Cookie sat at Gio's feet. The music was a lovely Christmas ballad, and Gio held out a hand to Sacha.

"Sway with me?"

Sacha laughed softly. "Okay."

Gio told Cookie to go with Duchess, and Cookie trotted over to where she lay in a fluffy bed on the side of the room. He lay down next to her, head on his paws, as he watched his daddies join the other couples on the dance floor. Gio brought his beautiful boyfriend into his arms, sighing contently when Sacha rested his head against Gio's chest.

They moved together, the night seeming to take

on a magical feel with all the twinkling lights and glittering Christmas trees around them. Snow fell outside the large arched windows, and the lights dimmed, creating an intimate atmosphere. By then, the families with children had left for the night.

Near them, Fitz and Jack danced together, and when Jack turned, Fitz winked at them over Jack's shoulder. Gio smiled. He had no doubt Fitz had been there for Sacha throughout all this. The two were close, though Gio wondered if even Fitz had known Sacha had been worried about Gio missing his traveling days.

Gio had meant everything he'd said to Sacha. Yes, he sometimes missed traveling, but his life had changed, and he was all the happier for it. Now, wherever he went, he wanted all three of his boys at his side, and he couldn't wait to see where their adventures took them.

CHAPTER SIX

"What is he up to? And how has no one figured it out yet?"

Joker frowned as he sat on the living room couch, watching Leo and Jack haul a bunch of tech equipment outside into one of the SUVs. There was no such thing as a secret in this family. Not with Ace. Someone had to know *something*.

"It *is* odd," Gio agreed from where he sat on the couch, his e-reader in one hand while he petted Cookie with the other. The Golden Retriever was out for the count, laying on his side with his head on Gio's lap, as opposed to his brother, who lay sprawled on the carpeted floor, paws up and back legs spread indecently as he snored away.

"He's been at this for weeks," Joker said. "What

could possibly take so long to put together? He hasn't asked anyone for help, and he hasn't said a word about it to King. It's just weird." Everyone had asked and offered to help Leo with whatever he was putting together. "I gotta admit, I'm kinda impressed he's been able to keep it under wraps this long."

A cold chill swept in from the open front door, and Joker shivered. When he woke up this morning, he'd decided to have breakfast downstairs with everyone instead of in bed. He was *not* a rest-in-bed-all-day kind of person.

Afterward, he made himself comfortable on the huge couch in the living room with his tablet, knowing that he'd inevitably get dragged to whatever festive fun his brethren were taking part in.

Fitz appeared with a ginormous knit blanket and wrapped it around him. He opened his mouth to grumble his thanks to Fitz when Laz appeared on his other side, making him jump. *What the—* How did they keep popping up out of nowhere? Was Ace giving them lessons or something? *Fucking hell.*

"I made you some hot cocoa," Laz said cheerfully, handing Joker a bright red mug with a mountain of whipped cream and chocolate shavings.

"Thanks." He'd been about to take a sip when Colton walked by, stopping long enough to lift

Joker's leg and place a pillow under his cast. Joker moved his gaze to his boyfriend, who had his head turned away, shoulders shaking. "Oh my god, you're laughing!"

Gio threw his head back against the couch cushions, his laughter filling the room.

"You shit! You're enjoying this." If he wasn't holding a steaming hot mug of chocolate deliciousness, he would have grabbed the nearest cushion and smacked his boyfriend with it.

Gio shook his head but couldn't talk because he was *laughing. His. Ass. Off.*

"Unbelievable," Joker grumbled. "And this is the man I plan to marry one day. Ass." He snorted and scooped up a bunch of whipped cream with his finger, popping it into his mouth. Damn, this was good. Did Red make the whipped cream? Wait. Why was the room so quiet all of a sudden?

Joker lifted his gaze and found *everyone* in the living room. Where the holly hell had they all come from? Had they been hiding, waiting to pop out to scare the shit out of him? And why were they standing there frozen, gaping at him?

"What?" Joker asked. He touched his nose. Had he gotten whipped cream on his face without knowing?

"Um," Ace darted his gaze around the room. "You all heard it, right? It wasn't a hallucination?" He grabbed Colton's hand and put it to his forehead. "Baby, do I have a fever?"

"No," Colton said slowly, eyes still on Joker.

"What? What the fuck is wrong with you all?" He looked at Gio, who sat there staring at him, his face flushed and his eyes glassy. "Oh, my god, what's wrong?" Joker glared at Ace. "What did you do?"

Ace choked on air. "*Me*? I didn't do anything! You're the one who broke him! And us. You broke us. We're broken." He grabbed Colton's arm, whispering loudly. "I don't know what to do or say. Help me! I can't think of words! Car, dog, eellogofusciouhipoppokunurious!"

Joker gasped. "What the fuck just came out of your mouth, Anston? Are you speaking in tongues? Should we call a priest?" Was no one else as terrified as he was right now?

"It's his newest Scrabble word," Colton replied calmly. "It means very good."

"Then why didn't he just say very good? Does that even fit on the board? Never mind." Joker put his mug on the coffee table and shifted so he could check on Gio. "Baby? What's wrong?"

"We should go," Colton said.

"But—" Ace was shoved toward the kitchen, everyone hurrying after them.

Why was his family so weird?

Joker took Gio's hand in his. "Gio? Talk to me."

"You really don't know what you said?"

Joker pursed his lips. "That my family is so weird? No, wait, I thought that." What had he said? Gio had been laughing, and Joker called him an ass and—

"Holy fucking shitballs!"

"There it is," Gio said, laughing softly. "You really want to get married one day?"

Joker worried his bottom lip and sighed. "You know the night I ran after Chip? I said he had something in his mouth?"

Gio nodded.

"I wasn't chasing him. He was chasing me. The stall next to the one we were at had wedding bands, and I glanced at one of the rings and suddenly got a picture of us getting married, and...well, um...."

"You panicked."

Joker was very glad Gio wasn't mad or disappointed. "Yeah. And then Jack showed up and we talked. The funny thing is, after thinking about it, it wasn't the marrying you part that made me panic, but the, uh, wedding part."

Gio blinked at him. "The wedding?"

"Yep. I thought about what Ace and Colton went through, and I won't lie to you, baby. The idea of having to work out seating arrangements for hundreds of people and being asked to pick out colors and flowers makes me break out in hives." He put a hand to his chest. "I'm getting heart palpitations just thinking about it, and not in a good way. I might need to lie down."

The last thing Joker expected was for Gio to throw his arms around him and hug him tight. "I love you so damned much, Sacha Wilder."

"You're not upset?"

Gio pulled back and shook his head. "Of course not. Do you really think any of that means more than just having you as my husband?"

Joker blinked at him. "Really? Because you can be honest with me. We can work it out." And he truly believed that.

Gio's smile stole Joker's breath away. Or maybe it was the thought of having to pick out a cake. He brushed that thought aside and leaned in to Gio's touch, sighing at the feel of Gio's fingers tenderly brushing his hair away from his brow and then caressing his cheek.

"Sweetheart, I promise you, whatever happens,

what matters to me most is you and our family. I love you." He leaned in to whisper, his voice husky. "I need you upstairs, in bed, under me. Right now."

Joker swallowed hard. He nodded and stood so quickly that Chip rolled to his feet and jumped up with a bark. "Sorry, boy. Daddy's about to get some, so you need to stay."

"Ugh, I did not need to hear that," Ace shouted from the kitchen.

"Then you shouldn't have been eavesdropping!" Joker grabbed his crutches and hurried to the stairs. When they got upstairs and locked the door behind them, they tore at each other's clothes. Gio sucked on Joker's neck, and his knees went weak.

"Oh, fuck," Joker growled.

"Get on the bed."

Joker stepped back, his breath hitching as he took in all of Gio's glorious nakedness. Damn, he was fine. He shook his head. "*You* get on the bed." He wrapped a hand around Gio's hard, leaking cock, loving Gio's sharp intake of breath. "Because I'm gonna ride you. *Hard.*"

Gio cursed under his breath, and when Joker released him, he darted over to the bed. Joker removed the lube from the nightstand drawer, then carefully climbed up, mindful of not whacking Gio with his cast or hurting himself as he straddled him. With a wicked grin, he leaned in and sucked Gio's bottom lip into his mouth.

"Stretch my hole."

Gio groaned and threw his head back. "Fuck."

"Yes. Fuck. That's exactly what you're going to do to me." Joker put the bottle of lube in Gio's hand. "Let's go, future husband. My ass is getting cold."

Gio laughed and cupped the back of Joker's neck, bringing him down for a scorching kiss. "I love you so damned much."

Joker smiled against Gio's lips. "I know."

With a playful growl, Gio poured some lube onto his hand and did exactly what Joker asked him to, using his long fingers to stretch Joker until he was a sweaty, panting mess that couldn't take it anymore. He moved Gio's hand and lined Gio's cock up with his hole, then biting his bottom lip, he slowly sank down until he was seated on Gio's groin.

Joker hummed at how full and stretched he was. He leaned slightly forward and placed his hands on Gio's chest, groaning when Gio grabbed hold of his asscheeks, parting them as Joker started moving.

"Oh fuck, Gio." Joker pulled almost all the way off, then drove himself down hard. He did it again and again, his ass bouncing against Gio's groin as he fucked himself on Gio's cock. Those strong hands moved to Joker's waist, and Gio planted his feet on the bed, his knees bent as he met Joker's ass with deep, hard thrusts. "Fuck yeah, baby. Just like that."

Gio adjusted his position, and when he punched his hips, Joker saw stars.

"Holy fuck!" Joker grabbed his own leaking cock and pumped himself, his hand matching Gio's moves as he drove himself into Joker over and over, the sounds of their bodies smacking together music to Joker's ears. Heat flooded through his body, his skin feeling as if it was on fire. How could he have possibly believed, even for a second, that anyone other than him belonged with Gio?

In a few short years, Joker had gone from swearing he'd never fall in love to giving himself so completely to this amazing man. "I'm gonna come," Joker warned. His orgasm slammed into him, and he doubled over, his come hitting Gio's chest. He trembled from how hard he came, his muscles tensing and tightening around Gio.

Gio cursed, his hips moving wildly as he pounded Joker's ass. He cried out, liquid heat filling Joker and making him groan. When he carefully pulled out, Joker rolled onto the bed on his side next to Gio, both of them laying there panting, trying to catch their breath.

"You okay, baby?" Joker asked softly, brushing his fingers down Gio's arm. Although there hadn't been any issues after sex as of yet, Joker always checked to make sure Gio was okay.

"Better than," Gio promised. "I am sticky, though. How about we take a shower?"

"I like that idea." Joker hummed as he rolled onto his stomach and peppered kisses up Gio's shoulder. He felt...light. Next time he started freaking out about something, he'd slow his roll and remember this was Gio. All they had to do was talk it through. And since when was he the kind of guy who freaked out about anything? Then again, this was the first time he had someone he loved so deeply who he wanted to share his life with.

Gio got up, and Joker followed. It took a little longer than usual for them to get in the shower because they had to get Joker's leg wrapped in the plastic, waterproof sock thing that was incredibly annoying. As soon as they were done, they got into the shower, which led to more fooling around and Gio on his knees. When they were dry and dressed, they went back downstairs.

Joker went into the kitchen to grab them a couple

of water bottles. He sighed as he closed the fridge door. Ace stood on the other side.

"Really?"

"How'd you know I was here?" Ace asked.

"There was a disturbance in the Force."

Ace laughed. "And you say Jack is a nerd."

"Where is everyone?" Joker asked, walking into the living room and handing Gio one of the water bottles.

"Leo went to help Santa—whatever *that* means. The dogs are all upstairs in the movie room with Laz, and I'm heading out to join the others to help Luz find Juniper."

"I don't know what those words mean," Joker said. "Who are Luz and Juniper?"

"Luz is the owner of the Jingle Paws stall," Gio replied, looking concerned. "Juniper is her Irish Setter, remember?"

"Oh shit. I remember them." They'd met the happy pair the night Joker had his little freakout. Oh no. "Wait, they're out there searching for Juniper, and the sniffer dog is upstairs?"

Ace shrugged. "No one knows how to do what you do with Chip. That's why you do it, and you two were, uh, indisposed."

Joker sighed. "Do we have a car?"

"The SUV is outside. Lucky and Mason took one of the snowmobiles from the garage, and Jack took the other one."

"Okay, let's go," Joker said, heading for the door. He texted Laz to let Chip and Cookie out so they could go with them to search for Juniper. Well, Chip would do most of the searching, but after last night, Joker didn't want Gio going anywhere without Cookie. "We're wasting daylight."

The sound of thumping paws on the stairs was followed by Laz. He carried a dozing Cocoa in his arms, Duchess at his side.

"Be careful," Laz said. "Let me know if there's anything I can do."

"Thanks for looking after the pups," Ace said as they headed for the door.

"No problem."

"Wait." Gio darted off upstairs and returned with the snow cast cover he had shipped in. "You're going to need this."

"Thanks, babe." Joker kissed his cheek and then quickly helped Gio get the dogs into their winter coats and boots. As soon as the dogs were ready, they followed Ace out to the SUV. "Let's go find us a missing dog."

CHAPTER SEVEN

Watching Sacha and Chip work was incredible.

The circumstances were terrible, but Gio rarely got to watch his boys at work, mostly because whenever Sacha and Chip did their searches, it was for an event that Four Kings Security had been hired for. When they'd first started dating, Gio had asked Sacha a million questions about how they did what they did.

Sacha had explained that for Chip, it was a game. He knew if he found the thing Sacha wanted him to find, he'd get a reward. Chip loved nothing more than having a job to do. There was a lot of scent work involved, and he'd been trained to sniff out all the different types of scents associated with explosives.

Like most dogs, Chip's sense of smell was so finely tuned that he smelled individual components rather than just the thing. He didn't smell the device itself, he smelled everything that made up the device —wires, individual chemicals, plastics, metals, rubber, all the pieces.

They texted King on the drive to town and met the others in the snow-covered field beyond the market square. Jack, Lucky, and Mason took the snowmobiles and searched ahead. Red came prepared with his medical bag, and the rest of the guys all had backpacks. King handed one to Gio.

"What's this?" Gio asked, taking the military-style bag.

"Hope for the best, prepare for the worst," King replied. "Never know what we're going to encounter, and this isn't the kind of terrain we're used to. I want everyone equipped."

Gio noticed a couple of the boyfriends weren't present. "Where are Fitz and Leo?"

"Leo is at the Ice Castle with Santa, helping him with who knows what, and Jack told Fitz to hang out at the coffee shop in case anyone needed anything. As much as Fitz wanted to help, we didn't want him out here in this cold for hours. It'd be too much for him."

King wasn't wrong. Gio was surprised at how much time Fitz had spent outdoors as it was, though he was certain *many* layers were involved.

Gio slipped his arms into the backpack and turned to see Sacha talking to Luz. He was clearly reassuring her. The poor girl was on the verge of bursting into tears. She handed Sacha a pink blanket with hearts and paw prints on it. He called Colton over, and Colton wrapped an arm around Luz's shoulders, murmuring to her as they walked toward the market square.

With Cookie at his side, Gio walked over to Sacha, who held the blanket out to Chip.

"Such und Gib Laut," Sacha ordered, and Chip took off, running at full speed until he was a black and red speck in a sea of white. They'd decided to dress both dogs in their red winter coats and boots so they could be seen more easily in the snow. Cookie was in work mode, so he remained beside Gio, watching his brother off in the distance.

"What did you say?" Gio asked, knowing Sacha had given some kind of German command.

"Search and bark. When he finds whatever this scent belongs to, he'll bark to let us know he's found it." Sacha turned to his brothers. "Let's move out. Someone text Jack, Lucky, and Mason, and tell them to keep an eye out for Chip."

"I'm on it," Ace replied.

They headed into the woods in the direction Chip had disappeared. Searching also meant tracking, something the Kings and the Wild Cards were very good at, though, as King had said earlier, the snowy terrain made everything more challenging. Thankfully, they were all bundled up from head to toe and wearing heavy winter boots.

As they followed the trail Chip made in the snow, some of them called for Juniper. Much of the ground in the woods was untouched, with inches of pristine white snow, while other parts had tracks from various animals. The woods were thick with trees, and littered with fallen logs, tree stumps, branches, and snow-covered boulders. It was damned cold, but the bright sun in the sky helped, especially when it shone through the trees.

Gio had no idea how long they'd been searching, and he was starting to worry. So far, they hadn't heard anything from Chip or the others on the snowmobiles. Just when Gio was about to ask if maybe they should split up and spread out, Cookie whined. At hearing Cookie, Sacha stilled.

"Stop."

They all stopped and listened. Gio could hear it!

"It's Chip," Gio said excitedly. The barking was faint, but they could hear it up ahead. They all hurried, the barks growing louder as they approached a densely wooded area. When they got close enough, they could see Chip next to a fallen tree, tail wagging as he barked and dug in the snow. As they approached, they heard more whining, but this time it wasn't Cookie.

"It's Juniper," Ace said, hurrying over. He bent over, looked in the tree, then straightened. "She's stuck."

"She probably chased a squirrel in there," Sacha said, praising Chip for a job well done. He ran over excitedly to get his reward, and Sacha gave Chip a lot of love and then treats from the baggie in his coat pocket.

"How are we going to get her out?" Gio asked.

King removed his backpack and took out what looked like a small cordless handsaw. Had he brought that with him for this particular situation, or did he always just have a handsaw at the ready? One never knew with the Kings.

"Is that safe?" Gio murmured to Sacha.

"Oh yeah. King will carefully cut into the log

until it's as close to Juniper as possible without actually going through the log. Then he'll use a chisel to start breaking the thing open. Eventually, we'll be able to pull it apart enough for her to back out."

"It sounds like you've all done this before."

Sacha glanced at him. "We have experience with search and rescue."

When his boyfriend didn't elaborate, Gio knew it was related to their time in the military, so he didn't ask. Sacha told him as much as he could. A lot of what he and his unit had done while they served was still classified.

Gio hydrated while King and Ace carefully cut Juniper free from the log. When she was finally out, she was excited and happy, her mouth open and her tail wagging so hard her entire butt moved. She made her way to each one of them, finally stopping beside Sacha who held her blanket.

"Let's head back and return Juniper to her person," King said when his phone rang. He removed it from his pocket and answered. "Hey, Jack. We found Juniper. She—*What*?"

The way King went stiff sent a chill through Gio.

Something was wrong.

"Where? Okay, we're close by. Heading to you now."

"What happened?" Ace asked.

"Move out," King ordered, and everyone took off after him. "A deer jumped out in front of Mason and Lucky's snowmobile. Mason swerved, and they ended up on a frozen pond. The weight of the snowmobile caused cracks all over the ice. Ace, Lucky fell in."

Ace didn't respond. Instead, he picked up speed and outran them. Gio turned to Sacha, who shook his head and waved an arm. "Go. I'll catch up."

Gio hurried after the others, Cookie and Chip running alongside him. As they got closer, Gio saw Jack. He was running toward the pond and shouting at Mason, who was slipping and sliding across the ice. Gio's heart pounded in his ears as Mason kicked at a spot in the ice and fell through.

"Oh my god!" Gio ran with the others toward the pond. A heartbeat later, Mason popped up, Lucky in his arms. Everyone ran onto the pond, including Gio, but King ordered him to stay back, and Gio understood. He stopped near the edge, Sacha caught up not long after. The guys spread out so their weight wasn't all in the same spot, then they got on their knees and reached into the water. They pulled Mason and Lucky out, dragging them to a more solid section of the ice where Red waited.

Sacha clipped Juniper to Chip in case she tried to run off again. He ordered the dogs to stay before he made his way out onto the ice, and Gio followed. It was slippery, but their boots and the snow on the ice helped a little with the traction. They'd just reached the others when Lucky made a horrible gurgling sound. Red rolled him onto his side, and Lucky coughed up a mouthful of water.

"We need to get them indoors and in some dry clothes," Red said, pulling thermal blankets from his bag. King and Ace quickly wrapped up Lucky while Red wrapped a blanket around Mason.

"What the fuck did you think you were doing, Cowboy?" King growled as he and Ace helped Lucky to his feet.

Mason stood, shivering, his scowl deep. "I was thinking the man I love fell through the fucking ice, and the devil himself wasn't gonna stop me from getting to him. Don't act like you would have done different."

King didn't argue because they all knew Mason was right. Any one of them would have done the same. Jack had removed a rope and a weird-looking ax that Gio realized had to be some kind of ice ax. Red carried a wrapped-up Lucky to Jack's snowmobile while the guys used the rope and ax to carefully drag the other snowmobile off the ice. As soon as they had, Mason headed to that one with Jack. Gio was sure if Mason hadn't been soaking wet and shivering violently, he would have been climbing on with Lucky. Instead, he let Red take Lucky and rode with Jack.

"Meet us at Urgent Care," Red called out as the engines roared to life. They took off toward town. Ace turned to King, who motioned for Ace to follow.

"You go ahead. I'll text Fitz and ask him to bring the boys some warm clothes."

"Thanks. I'll see you guys there," Ace said and took off after them.

Now that the worst of the danger was over, Gio felt a little shaky. He wasn't going to say anything because, for fuck's sake, they'd just been through one hell of a scare, but Cookie whined and poked Gio's leg. Sacha pointed to a stump near the trees.

"Sit down."

Gio did as he was told and closed his eyes, remembering to breathe.

"Here. Drink this as soon as you're able."

Opening his eyes, Gio took the bottle of water and the pill Sacha held out. In the early days of his diagnosis, he'd been embarrassed every time he'd had an episode, but Sacha helped him understand and accept that sometimes his body just didn't work the way it should, and it was nothing for him to be ashamed of or embarrassed about.

It took some time for Gio to stop apologizing for his condition, and when he did, he realized that he was the only one who hadn't accepted his new limitations.

King walked over. "I know this gave you one hell of a scare. Scared the shit out of the rest of us too." He shook his head. "Cowboy was probably losing his damned mind."

Gio doubted Mason had given it a second thought before jumping in after Lucky. But King was right. As scared as the rest of them had been, poor Mason must have been terrified.

Gio drank down the bottle of water, and once the dizziness wore off, he stood. Between Sacha walking with crutches and Gio being mindful of his pace, it took some time for them to get back to town. By then, Red had texted King to let him know Lucky and Mason were okay. According to the doctor, Mason's quick—albeit foolish—reaction had saved Lucky. Fitz had taken them some warm, dry clothes, and they were waiting for the pair to be released, so there was no need for everyone to crowd the Urgent Care waiting room.

King said he'd return Juniper to Luz and insisted Sacha take Gio back to the cabin. Gio didn't argue. They arrived at the cabin before the others and found Laz in the living room with Cocoa and Duchess.

"Red called. I'm so glad they're okay," Laz said, letting out a sigh of relief. "I can't imagine what you all must have been feeling out there. And poor Mason." He shook his head. "But they're safe now. Oh, and Fitz called. He's going to pick up dinner from the Festive Spruce Diner for everyone. I think some hot comfort food is in order."

"I think you're right," Gio said, hanging up all their outerwear. He removed Cookie's coat. "Off duty." Cookie immediately joined the others in play.

"Speaking of food. It's time to feed the beasts," Sacha said as he walked into the kitchen. The moment he opened the pantry, the furry hoard descended. Of course, Sacha had taught all of them dinner manners—even Cocoa—so they sat in a line at one end of the kitchen.

Sacha prepared all four dog food bowls, and once he finished—one at a time—he put a bowl down, called a dog over, and gave the word for them to eat. All except for Cocoa. Sacha handed Cocoa's bowl to Laz, who hand-fed the puppy. Hand feeding helped

Cocoa build a relationship with his people and learn trust. It also stopped him from inhaling his kibble.

By the time the dogs had eaten, everyone started trickling in. They helped Fitz get the dinner table ready. When Mason and Lucky arrived, everyone made a fuss and hugged them. Red figured they'd want to take their dinner upstairs, so he'd prepared them two covered plates. It had been one hell of a day, and everyone was physically and mentally done.

After dinner, Colton sat on the couch, Ace stretched out beside him, his head on Colton's lap, asleep.

"Leave it," Sacha told Chip.

They both knew Chip would have dive-bombed Ace otherwise.

"I didn't expect him to be asleep," Gio whispered to Sacha as they made their way upstairs. Considering how close Ace and Lucky were, he'd half expected Ace to have been hovering over his cousin.

"Everyone handles extreme stress differently. In our case, we're trained to react, and back when we served, if we were facing an extremely stressful or dangerous situation, we got an adrenaline rush and became more alert because that's how you survive. Now, we just crash. Also, I get the feeling that if he tries to smother Lucky tonight, he's going to get a cowboy boot up his ass."

Gio chuckled. "That makes more sense."

As they closed the bedroom door behind them and watched the dogs trot over to their beds beneath the window, Gio was glad to be home. It had been one hell of a day. Time to change into his pajamas and crawl into bed with his beautiful boyfriend.

As he lay propped against his pillows, his arm around Sacha, who lay snuggled against him, and a Christmas movie on TV, their dogs decided they didn't want to be left out. They darted over and jumped on the bed, dropping onto the mattress at Sacha's back, and were fast asleep in seconds. Gio's heart swelled with pride and love. He would cherish this moment. The jingling of sleigh bells coming from the TV, the snow falling outside their window, and the faint scent of cinnamon had Gio drifting off to sleep with a smile on his face.

CHAPTER EIGHT

"¡M adrecita, mía, Ace! I'm fine!"
And so it begins.

Joker glanced up from where he sat on the floor with Cocoa. He couldn't see the cousins, but he sure as shit could hear them. People all the way in town could probably hear them. How was Mason still asleep? Then again, he was dating Lucky, so he was probably used to it by now. Sounded like Ace and Lucky were coming downstairs.

"You could have died!"

Cocoa popped his head up when he heard his daddy. "Brace yourself, buddy," Joker warned, laughing when Cocoa let out a little whine and tilted his head, one ear flopping against the other. Ugh, he loved those puppy ears.

Gio was still out with Fitz. The two had taken Cookie, Chip, and Duchess for a walk while Joker stayed behind to do a little training with Cocoa. Ace was supposed to have been training with them, but he'd disappeared a while ago, and now Joker knew where he'd gone. To annoy the shit out of Lucky.

"I'm sorry I scared you, but I'm fine now, so you can stop trying to suffocate me. Like, literally. I couldn't breathe under the ten sherpa blankets you covered me in. And why were you even in our room, bro?"

"I was checking on you," Ace replied with a huff.

"We were sleeping! That's just weird. Stop being weird!"

Joker snorted. *Yeah, that ship has sailed, pal.* It was somewhere in the Bermuda Triangle and never coming back.

Ace rounded the couch after Lucky. "Eduardo Morales, let me take care of you!"

With a snicker, Joker lifted Cocoa. "That's right. Your daddy's a giant dork. Get used to it."

"I cannot have you and the Boyfriends trying to take care of me. I won't survive." Lucky tried to run when Ace threw his arms around him from behind to stop him.

"Why won't you let me love you!"

"Stop it. Damn it, Ace. No, don't do the thing. Don't—¡Me cago en diez!"

Ace let himself go limp so he was dead weight, his arms still around Lucky's waist. Lucky tried to walk, dragging Ace with him. Joker looked around the room. Why was no one recording this? Then again, he doubted Colton wanted evidence of his husband's ridiculousness, and King, well, he was King.

The cousins started shouting at each other in Spanish, and Joker held back a laugh. Ace hadn't just gone into protective mother-hen mode. He'd gone into Cuban mother levels of protective mode, and it was terrifying. Good thing they weren't back home because if they had been, the Cuban Mama Mafia would have been on the first flight from Miami to St. Augustine.

"Go back to trying to take care of Joker," Lucky growled. "He is still injured. Which, by the way, is kind of your fault."

"What? You asshole! I can't believe you're throwing me under the bus!" Joker said.

"Better you than me, bro."

Ace's phone rang, and he reached into his pocket, his other arm still around Lucky. He looked at the screen and gasped. "Fuck, it's your mother! Why is your mother calling me?"

Lucky shrugged. "I don't know. Maybe because she's your aunt?"

Bullshit.

"And she's *your* mother." Ace gasped again. "You fuck! She called you, and you didn't answer her call? Are you *high*?"

If there was one thing Joker had learned about the Cuban Mama Mafia—besides the fact that they believed no one ever ate enough and that everything could be solved with food—was that they had an instinct for when their boys were hurt or sick. He'd also learned you didn't ignore their calls. That way lay madness.

Colton's phone rang and vibrated across the coffee table. He stared at it like it might spring up and attack him any second. "Lucky, your mother is calling me."

"For fuck's sake, someone answer her call," Lucky said, trying to get out of Ace's iron grip.

"How about *you* answer her call," Colton said, holding out his phone. "You're her son."

"You're her son-in-law," Lucky argued.

"For fuck's sake." King swiped Colton's phone,

ignoring Lucky and Ace's protest. He tapped the screen, and a woman's voice came over the speaker.

"Cariño, donde esta Candi?"

Lucky sighed and let his head fall forward. "Aquí, Mami."

"Eduardo! Why did you not pick up your phone? What is going on? Are you okay? Are you hurt? Where is Mason?"

"Esta durmiendo."

"¿Qué? Sleeping? At this time? What is wrong with him?"

Joker pressed his lips together to keep himself from making a sound. She couldn't know he was here because then someone would open their big annoying mouth and spill the beans on him being in a cast, and then he was fucked.

"He is not feeling well, Mami. I think he is getting a cold."

Nice! *Throw your sleeping boyfriend under the bus.* Joker approved.

Mrs. Morales tsked. "¡Ay, pobrecito! You take good care of him, Eduardo. Have you made him soup?"

"I was just on my way to do that. I should go do that," Lucky said, pointing to the kitchen as if she could see him.

"¿Dónde está Chulo?"

Lucky took a step forward, and Ace let himself slide to the floor. He rolled onto his back with a sigh. "Aqui, tía."

"Chulo! Why did you not answer your phone?"

"I'm sorry, tía. I was, uh...." Ace looked around the room. "I was in the middle of a puppy potty emergency. Did Mami tell you Colton got me a puppy for Christmas?"

And everyone in the living room let out a collective sigh. Lucky's mom was busy cooing and gushing over Cocoa, and Joker was slowly, quietly getting up. Not an easy task with his stupid cast. He made his way into the kitchen.

"Are you really going to make your chicken soup?"

Like Red, Lucky was an amazing cook, having learned from his mother and aunt, though he made Cuban food instead of Red's southern comfort food. Either way, it meant deliciousness.

"Yes." Lucky side-eyed him as he removed a giant pot from the cabinet.

"Are you making it for Mason, or...?"

"You are not subtle. No, I am going to make enough for everyone."

Yes!

"Is he really not feeling well?" Joker asked, climbing up onto one of the tall-ass wooden stools at the counter. Who were these things made for? His feet dangled.

Lucky moved around the kitchen, gathering supplies before removing ingredients from the fridge. "I think he was catching a cold before...." He stopped at the counter, his frown deep. "I can't believe he jumped in after me."

"Really?" Joker took a shortbread Christmas cookie from the plate Red somehow managed to keep full throughout the day. "Cause if ya look up the definition of lovesick fool, there's a picture of Mason Cooper."

Lucky chuckled. His smile faded. "What if something had happened to him because of me?"

"Nope." Joker bit off a chunk of cookie and waved the remaining headless reindeer at him. "Don't go down that road. You know better. You're okay, he's okay. Make him some soup. Take care of him. Like a normal person, not like your cousin."

Lucky snorted. "¡Dios mío! My god. That man." He shook his head. "I know it's because he loves us, but can he not kill me in the process of trying to take care of me?"

"Yeah, good luck with that."

Barking announced the return of Gio and Fitz, followed by three furry monsters stampeding into the kitchen. Joker laughed as they darted over to him, butts wiggling excitedly.

"Yeah, yeah. I'm happy to see you, too." He gave them scritches, then lifted his face for a kiss from Gio, humming when their lips touched. "Hi, baby."

"Mm, sweet." Gio stuck his hand under Joker's shirt, laughing when Joker yelped and shoved him away.

"You shit! Your hand is freezing!"

Gio's chuckle was evil as he went to the fridge and pulled out a gallon of milk.

"Just for that, you can make me a hot chocolate."

Ace walked into the kitchen with a wriggling Cocoa in his arms. He blinked at Joker, then barked out a laugh.

"What the fuck is so funny?" Joker asked.

Ace pointed at him. "You look like that Christmas elf."

"What?" Joker was so confused. "What are you —" He dropped his gaze to his red sweatpants, one leg tucked into his white cast, and his red and white T-shirt. "The fuck?" He narrowed his gaze at Ace. "Fuck you, Anston." Everyone laughed, and Joker crossed his arms over his chest. He glared at Fitz. "This is your doing."

Fitz arched an eyebrow at him. "You asked for sweatpants, I got you sweatpants. It was either red— which is very festive—or space tacos. Those were the choices."

"Really. In all of Winterhaven, those were the only options available?"

"Honey, *all* of Winterhaven is one street. It has two clothing stores, and one is for children." Fitz snapped his fingers. "Damn. I should have gone into the children's store. Bet they had more choices."

Everyone burst into laughter again, and Joker flipped them all off. "Screw you all. Bunch of tall bastards." He pushed himself off the stool, ignoring his annoying family laughing as he hopped down and gathered his crutches. "I'm going upstairs to change. I need to go into town."

"For non-elf-sized clothes?" Ace asked.

"Don't you have a cousin to harass?" Joker turned to Fitz. "You and Jack wanna come with?"

"Ooh, shopping! We'll meet you down here," Fitz said, floating off to find his boyfriend. Joker went upstairs to change, Gio following him, and the dogs stampeding up the stairs behind them.

Getting any kind of pants on and off over his cast

was a pain in the ass. Joker sat on the bed while Gio helped him out of his very red sweatpants that now and forever would remind him of a certain shelf-sitting Christmas elf. Damn it, now he had to burn these.

The one thing Joker would not permit in his home was dolls. They creeped the shit out of him. Gio had a few dollish-type souvenirs from his travel days, but they weren't doll enough to break Joker's rule.

"I would rather invite Pennywise into my house than that demon elf," Joker grumbled.

Gio chuckled. "It does kind of look like it's up to something."

"Yeah, it's waiting for you to go to sleep so it can murder you. I swear if you stare at one long enough, its head will start spinning."

As soon as his pants were off, Gio returned with a pair of black cargo pants. He carefully lifted Joker's cast, then paused.

"What?" Joker asked.

"Um." Gio stared down at Joker's cast.

"Gio."

"You have a drawing on your cast. It's on the bottom of your foot."

"What the fuck? When did that happen?" Joker

tried to think of when any of his asshole brothers could have possibly gotten close enough to his cast with a marker without him knowing. He shook his head. "Never mind." He groaned. "What is it?" Did he want to know? No. Did he *have* to know? Yes.

Gio glanced at him, then the drawing, then back at Joker. "I don't think I should say."

"I bet it was Ace. Fucker. When the hell did he do it?" The thought was terrifying. He had to have been asleep when it happened, but how had he not felt it? "Just tell me."

"I could be wrong, but it looks like...a stick figure with a top hat."

Joker narrowed his eyes. That couldn't be all. "And...?"

"And it's also a penis. It's a penis with a top hat and stick figure arms and legs." Gio tilted his head to one side. "It's kind of cute."

Joker dragged his hands over his face with a loud groan. "I'm going to murder him in his sleep, and then I'm gonna steal his puppy."

Gio stood and kissed the tip of Joker's nose. "You're so darn cute when you're plotting someone's demise." He laughed at Joker's grunt and finished helping him get dressed. When they got downstairs, Ace was nowhere to be seen.

Colton sat stretched out on the couch with his laptop on his thighs. He didn't even bother looking up. "He ran the second he heard you coming. I'm guessing you found the penis."

"Wait, you knew about it, and you didn't tell me?"

Colton lifted his gaze. "My husband might be a giant man-child, but he's my husband." He dropped his gaze back to his laptop. "Also, his mom and Lucky's mom are coming to stay with us for a week after New Year's, so murdering him now is out of the question. Once they leave, he's all yours."

Joker threw back his head and laughed. "Oh my god, this is *amazing*!" He turned to Gio, his smile huge. "Did you hear that? The moms are staying at his house! Vengeance is mine, baby! This is going to be glorious." And yes, also terrifying, but Joker wasn't staying under the same roof. He could pop in, get fed delicious Cuban food, let them make a fuss over him and tell him how adorable he was, and then bounce. He wiped an imaginary tear from his eye. "I'm so happy." Turning to Colton, he put a hand to his heart. "I'm sorry. But you brought this on yourself. You married him. Bye."

"I heard that," Ace called out from the second floor. "Asshole!"

Joker cackled all the way out the front door. "Watch the dogs!"

Best. Christmas. Ever.

Jack climbed into the driver's side of the SUV, and Fitz got in the passenger side while Joker, Gio, and Cookie climbed into the back. They drove down to town, and Joker couldn't help but admire how great the main street looked. It felt good, knowing he'd had a hand in restoring it.

Originally, he'd volunteered so he could ride in the knuckle boom, but seeing the garland and the twinkling lights on the buildings was more satisfying than he expected. The sound of jingling bells and Christmas music filled various parts of town, all the shops were lit up and decorated, and the entire square smelled of gingerbread and cinnamon.

Joker left one of his crutches in the car to make getting around town a little easier. They strolled down the busy main street, and Joker smiled when Gio took his hand. It was nice. They never really got to stroll anywhere back home. Mostly because the humidity and sun were always trying to set you on fire. His having to walk using a crutch made him slow down, and he took his time looking through the shop windows.

"Are you looking for something in particular?" Gio asked.

"Nope."

Not a lie, exactly. He wasn't looking for a particular thing, but he *was* looking for something, he just didn't know what. But he'd know it when he saw it, and he couldn't wait.

CHAPTER NINE

Sacha was definitely looking for something.

They walked through town, stopping in shops, mostly to browse or buy trinkets for friends. Fitz bought a few things, and Jack even picked up some gifts for his team. Sacha remained on the hunt.

Back at the cabin, the bottom of the Christmas tree was packed with presents, though the majority of them were for the dogs, which Gio found amusing. The pups got enough toys and treats from family and friends to last them until the next Christmas.

"Oh! Brightly Books," Fitz said excitedly. He grabbed Jack's arm. "We *have* to go into the bookstore."

Jack chuckled. "Okay. Maybe think about

buying paperbacks instead of hardcovers this time? Not sure how many I can carry back to the car."

"*No promises*," Fitz sing-songed as he all but skipped into the bookstore.

Shaking his head, Jack opened the door for the rest of them. "Even if he doesn't buy anything, which is unlikely, he *loves* bookstores. Used to spend most of his childhood in them."

"Me too," Sacha replied. "Well, the library, mostly."

Gio was surprised. "Really?" He and Cookie followed Sacha into the bookstore. It was more spacious on the inside than Gio expected, cozy, with worn leather seating and old wood bookshelves lining the walls. There were tables piled high and stacks of books everywhere.

"When I was in foster care, I'd go to the library so I wouldn't have to go home. It was awesome. Warm or cool, depending on the time of year. Loads of free stuff to read, comfy couches, and beanbag chairs. Plus, the librarians loved me. They thought I was adorable, so they brought me juice and cookies, then they started bringing me food. A lot of the time, it's where I got most of my meals from. Before I met this delinquent," Sacha said, motioning to Jack.

Jack gave Gio a sad smile. When Sacha turned to

look at him, Jack's expression changed, and he smiled wide, giving Sacha a playful punch on the arm. "I think we all know who the delinquent was. I was an angel who could do no wrong."

Sacha snorted. "Yeah, your mom was the only one who believed that." He shook his head in shame. "She *still* thinks that. It's like she doesn't know you or something."

"Ass," Jack said with a laugh. He left to join Fitz, who already had half a dozen books in his arms, all hardcovers.

"Ooh, I don't have to carry anything this time," Sacha said. "*Sweet.* Fitz's book shopping will make you realize you do not work out as much as you should."

Gio chuckled, pretending his heart didn't hurt for Sacha. His boyfriend hated anyone feeling sorry for him. Gio felt a lot of things—rage, heartache, sadness—when he learned something new about Sacha's childhood. Sacha very rarely talked about his past or his childhood, but occasionally, he'd share something, and it always broke Gio's heart.

This beautiful man had been through so much, and here he stood, his eyes lighting up at the sight of a goldfish cracker plushie. He snatched it off the shelf and showed it to Gio.

"Oh my god, how has Leo not seen this?"

Gio shrugged. "I wonder if he's even been in here. He's been so busy with whatever he's doing. It's Christmas Eve. I hope he'll be done by tonight."

"Oh, I'm sure he will. Red's already texted everyone about tonight's family photo." He rolled his eyes. "Everyone has to dress up nice."

Every Christmas, Laz took photos of the family together, along with photos of each couple. Red made sure everyone dressed up, so he'd had everyone bring clothes in preparation for tonight. The moment the picture-taking was over, Sacha would be back in his T-shirt and sweatpants.

They spent a good deal of time in the bookstore, everyone finding something to take home. In Fitz's case, finding lots of somethings to take home. Gio had no idea Fitz was such a voracious reader. From the looks of his stack, he read everything from fantasy and romance to crime thrillers and biographies. Sacha, of course, bought the plushie for Leo.

"Let's put this stuff in the car," Jack said through a grunt as he walked out of the bookstore with several very heavy bags of books.

Sacha checked his watch. "We should grab some

lunch. Why don't we meet at the pub? Gio and I will get a table."

"Sounds good," Jack replied as he and Fitz headed off.

The pub was busy, but they were able to get a booth near the back by the fireplace and the tufted leather couch. Gio always tried to get a table out of the way or gave them more room. Although Cookie always remained close to him, Gio didn't want to take the chance that someone might not see Cookie and trip over him.

They ordered drinks, and shortly after, Fitz and Jack joined them. The pub reminded him of his travels through Europe. He couldn't wait to start making travel plans with Sacha. He'd bet Sacha would love Britain.

"I can't believe it's Christmas Eve," Fitz said, wrapping his arms around Jack and kissing his cheek. "This has been the best Christmas yet."

Sacha nodded. "Yeah, I kinda—"

At the sudden silence, Gio turned to look at Sacha. His boyfriend was staring in the direction of the bar.

"Are you okay?" Gio asked.

"Yeah, um...." Sacha cleared his throat. "I'm fine. Don't let your food get cold. I'll be right back." He got up, took his crutch, and made his way to the crowded bar.

"What's that about?" Jack asked, looking over his shoulder at Sacha who leaned against the bar talking to Clarence, the pub owner.

"It's Joker," Fitz said with a grin. "Who knows."

When Clarence smiled and nodded, Gio's tension eased. Whatever was going on wasn't something to worry about. Gio went back to eating and talking to the others. A few minutes later, Sacha returned to the table.

"Everything okay?" Gio asked.

"Yep. Just had to talk to Clarence about something."

"Okay." Jack and Fitz exchanged glances but didn't question him. If Sacha wanted them to know, he would have said something, but Gio was curious.

After lunch, they did a little more shopping and had some delicious hot chocolate and pastries from the bakery. Gio gave Cookie some more water and then, shortly after, took him for a potty break. When he returned, the lovely young man behind the counter gave Gio a Christmas doggy biscuit for Cookie.

"I'm going to miss this place," Fitz said, looking around.

"We can always come back," Jack replied, kissing the side of Fitz's head. "According to Clara, the town has all kinds of festivities and events year-round. There doesn't seem to be a shortage of things for them to celebrate."

Fitz clapped excitedly. "That would be so much fun!" He kissed Jack's cheek. "What do you think, Joker?"

Sacha shrugged. "I wouldn't be opposed to coming back here."

Which meant Sacha liked the town. Gio would keep that in mind. It would make a lovely little getaway. They got back to the cabin and hung out downstairs for a bit until it was time for dinner. Afterward, they all headed to their bedrooms to shower and get ready for their family photos. Sacha made Gio laugh by refusing to shower with him because he knew there would be "sexy shenanigans," and they didn't have time.

Gio walked out of the bathroom and stilled. "Oh." He couldn't help but stare at Sacha. The deep royal blue suit and the black dress shirt underneath were tailored for Sacha's petite frame, and he looked breathtaking. The suit made his eyes appear more blue than gray, and Gio found himself mesmerized. It was a rare occasion when Gio got to see Sacha dressed like this, so when it occurred, he couldn't help being left speechless.

"What?" Sacha looked down at himself. "I managed to get my pants on over my cast. I told Laz not to get it in the pictures. No one needs reminding that I was defeated by Ace and an extension cord."

Gio chuckled and walked over to his beautiful man. He wrapped him in his arms, careful not to wrinkle him. "You look stunning."

"Thanks. You look pretty damn good yourself." Sacha smiled and wrapped his arms around Gio's neck. He brushed his lips over Gio's. "You got the lint rollers ready?"

Gio laughed. "There are about half a dozen downstairs. Hopefully, Chip won't rip off his bow tie this time."

"Yeah, my boy's not a suit and tie kind of guy either," Sacha replied with a snort. "But Fitz insists they look their best, which is why I leave it to him. If he wants to wrestle that furry menace into submission, he's welcome to it."

"Speaking of submission," Gio teased, nipping at Sacha's ear.

"Oh no. Don't even think about, Giovanni. You have any idea what a pain in the ass it was to get into these pants?"

"And who says I have to take them off?" Gio slid his hand around Sacha's waist down to his ass and squeezed his cheeks, loving the way Sacha groaned. Then shook his head and gently pushed Gio back.

"No. Nope." Sacha held a hand up before Gio could protest. "And there's a reason for that. I have something for you."

Gio was pleasantly surprised. "Really?"

"Wait here." Sacha went over to his nightstand and pulled out a medium-sized gold box with a pretty gold ribbon tied around it. He carried it over to Gio. "I got this for you, and I want you to open it now instead of tomorrow in front of everyone."

Curious. When had Sacha gotten this for him? They'd been together practically the whole time. Gio's heart swelled as he took the box from Sacha, charmed by his flushed cheeks. Gio had no idea what could put that sweet look on his man's face. Gently pulling off the ribbon, he removed the lid, and his heart leaped into his throat.

"Oh, Sacha...."

"It's a promise," Sacha said as Gio removed the beautiful little box with the vintage-style globe inside. "A promise to make memories together anywhere in the world. You just point, and we'll go there together."

"This is the most amazing gift anyone has ever given me," Gio whispered as he ran a finger over the smooth globe. He would cherish this always. "Thank you." He placed his fingers under Sacha's chin and kissed him, a sweet and tender kiss. "I love you so much."

"I love you too," Sacha replied with a smile. "Merry Christmas, baby."

"Merry Christmas, love."

Fitz had been right. This had been the best Christmas yet, and Gio had never been happier. They might not have time to make love, but that didn't stop Gio from bringing Sacha into his arms and kissing him until they were forced to come up for air.

"We should go," Sacha said with a sigh.

Gio nodded. He placed the lid back on his gift box and carefully placed the box inside his nightstand, the possibilities of all the places they could go and memories they could make filling Gio's heart with warmth and excitement.

They'd just been about to leave the room when both their phones pinged with a text. Gio removed his phone and checked his messages.

"Jack says we're all meeting at the Ice Castle. The Blue Ballroom."

Sacha nodded. "Yeah, I got the same text. I guess Red decided to take photos there."

"Makes sense. It does look beautiful in there, and I suppose we should take advantage of Winterhaven's gorgeous scenery." The photos were going to be particularly stunning this year, and Gio was looking forward to finding the perfect photos to frame and hang up in their home.

Downstairs, some of the guys had already taken the first SUV down to the Ice Castle, including Red, Laz, Jack, Fitz, and Leo. No one questioned Red's decision. They just grabbed their coats and got into the second SUV.

"How come Leo went in the other SUV?" Sacha asked King as he climbed behind the wheel.

"He said Laz needed his help with one of his digital cameras. Something about some setting issues. To be honest, I have no idea what he was talking about. I barely know how to use my phone's camera, much less one of Laz's fancy cameras. Probably why Leo had his backpack with him."

Inside the SUV, Gio couldn't seem to keep his hands off Sacha, his heart was so happy.

"You're so smitten," Sacha teased quietly, leaning in to kiss Gio.

"I am," Gio agreed. How could he not be? Never

in his life had he expected to find someone like Sacha. Someone who loved so passionately, was fearless yet soft—even if he liked to think he wasn't—and who had the biggest heart of anyone Gio had ever known.

They arrived at the Ice Castle, and King parked the SUV. Inside, the guys were standing outside the Blue Ballroom. Laz removed his coat and gave it to Red so he could swing his digital camera's strap around his neck. He had his bag with all his lenses and equipment. Why hadn't they gone inside?

"We're here," Sacha grumbled. "Why are we all standing around?"

"Room's locked," Red said with a frown.

"Why? Didn't you make the arrangements?" Sacha asked.

Red looked confused. "What arrangements?"

Sacha eyed him. "What? You told Jack to text us to meet here."

"What?" Jack blinked at him. "I didn't know anything about this. I didn't text you either." He turned to Ace. "You're the one who told us to come here and 'dress nice.' What's this about, man?"

Ace blinked at him. "Um, I'm here because Red texted me. He's the one who wanted us all dressed up, remember? I figured we were taking our family photos here." Ace looked at Red. "Right?"

Red shook his head. "I didn't text you, and I didn't arrange any of this. But I thought it was a great idea. Colton was the one who came up with it. He messaged me."

"What?" Colton frowned. "I didn't text you."

Gio held a hand up. "Hold up. Did anyone send out a message asking to meet here?"

Nope.

"But everyone received a message to be here."

Yep.

"What the hell is going on?" King asked, looking around. "Wait. Where's Leo? Anyone see where Leo went?"

No one had any idea where Leo was or when he'd slipped away. King opened his mouth, and it seemed like he was going to say something about it, but instead, his brows drew together. "Clara?"

They all turned to see Clara dressed in a beautiful red and white dress. Was there some kind of party or event someone had forgotten to tell them about?

"Hello, boys. It's good to see you all."

"Do you know what's going on?" King asked. "We were asked to be here." He pointed to the name above the doors. "The Blue Ballroom. But it looks like it's closed. Also, have you seen Leo?" Just as he said the words, they heard the click of a lock.

"Oh, this room has been booked for a private event," Clara said cheerfully. "Everyone, remove your coats, please."

They all exchanged glances but did as they were asked, removing their coats to drape them over their arms.

"What event?" King asked.

Clara smiled sweetly, and just as she opened the doors, it hit everyone. The texts they received that none of them had sent, the dressing up, the fact Leo was missing, and how secretive he'd been....

Oh my god!

There was a collective gasp as Clara turned to King and patted his chest.

"We're here for your wedding, dear."

The ballroom looked like a magical Winter Wonderland, complete with ice sculpture reindeer, and at the end of the double aisles stood Leo dressed in a blue suit, his cheeks pink and a big boyish grin on his face. Next to him stood a big man with a white beard dressed in a red and white suit.

Santa.

Gio put a hand to his chest. "That's what he'd

been doing." He turned to King, who had tears in his eyes. Reaching out, Gio took King's coat from him. He looked so handsome in his black suit and royal blue dress shirt underneath. "Let's get you married, Ward."

King laughed softly and, with a nod, walked inside.

Sacha looked up at Gio and smiled. "Best. Christmas. Ever."

The Kings and Wild Cards holiday shenanigans continue with *Rebel without a Claus*, book 4 in The Kings: A Treemendous Christmas series.

A NOTE FROM THE AUTHOR

Thank you so much for reading *Home for the Howlidays*, the third book in The Kings: A Treemendous Christmas series. I hope you enjoyed Gio and Joker's holiday hijinks, and if you did, please consider leaving a review on Amazon.

The story continues in *Rebel without a Claus,* Book 4 in The Kings: A Treemendous Christmas series (Leo and King's holiday story), now available on Amazon and KU.

Reviews can have a significant impact on a book's visibility on Amazon, so any support you show these fellas would be amazing.

❋

Haven't read the Kings? Start with *Love in Spades*, available on Amazon and Kindle Unlimited.

Want to stay up-to-date on my releases and receive exclusive content? Sign up for my newsletter.

For exclusive content and to read select works-in-progress, join me on Patreon. Tiers start at $5 a month. The higher the tier, the more perks you receive, including ebooks, signed paperbacks, and exclusive merchandise!

Follow me on Amazon to be notified of a new releases, and connect with me on social media, including my fun Facebook group, Donuts, Dog Tags, and Day Dreams, where we chat books, post pictures, have giveaways, and more!

Looking for inspirational photos of my books? Visit my book boards on Pinterest.

Thank you again for visiting the Kings Universe. We hope to see you soon!

THIRDS Beyond the Books

THIRDS: Rebels

TIN

THIRDS Boxed Sets

OTHER SERIES AND NOVELS

Paranormal Princes Series

Soldati Hearts Series

North Pole City Tales Series

Love for the Reaper

DID YOU KNOW?

If you own a book or borrow it through Kindle Unlimited,
you can get Whispersynced audiobooks at a discounted
price. Interested in audio? Check out the Charlie Cochet
titles available on Audible.

ABOUT THE AUTHOR

Charlie Cochet is the international bestselling author of the THIRDS series. Born in Cuba and raised in the US, Charlie enjoys the best of both worlds, from her daily Cuban latte to her passion for classic rock.

Currently residing in Central Florida, Charlie is at the beck and call of a highly opinionated sable German Shepherd and a rascally Doxiepoo bent on world domination. When she isn't writing, she can usually be found devouring a book, releasing her creativity through art, or binge watching a new TV series. She runs on coffee, thrives on music, and loves to hear from readers.

www.charliecochet.com

Sign up for Charlie's newsletter:
https://newsletter.charliecochet.com

patreon.com/charliecochet

amazon.com/author/charliecochet

facebook.com/charliecochet

instagram.com/charliecochet

bookbub.com/authors/charliecochet

goodreads.com/CharlieCochet

pinterest.com/charliecochet

Made in the USA
Las Vegas, NV
15 December 2024

14264724R00083